S w e e t m e a t s

◇◇◇

Sport can be beautiful for so many reasons, as toned and limber athletes at the very peak of their performance demonstrate dedication and stamina on and off the field.

Inspired by this, we asked five erotic authors to demonstrate their literary prowess in this genre. Our authors did not disappoint, and they've delivered five wonderful stories of athletes who work hard and play harder. From the elegance and strength of the gymnast in training, to the speed and heat of the Formula One racetrack, precision and excellence always yield satisfying results! Come and join us as we explore and enjoy the *Athletic Aesthetic!*

A Sweetmeats Book

First published by Sweetmeats Press 2015

Copyright © Sweetmeats Press 2015

2 4 6 8 10 9 7 5 3 1

ISBN 978-1-909181-45-8

Typeset by Sweetmeats Press
Printed and bound in the U.S.

Sweetmeats Press
27 Old Gloucester Street, London, WC1N 3XX, England, U. K.
www.sweetmeatspress.com

ATHLETIC AESTHETIC

compiled by

KOJO BLACK

"In love as in sport, the amateur status must be strictly maintained."

—Robert Graves (1895 – 1985)

Contents

RIGOROUS TRAINING

LISA FOX

Rigorous Training

Chapter One

Christy scowled at the GPS unit on her dashboard. Stupid technology. She had been on this single-lane country road for miles upon miles and there was no civilization in sight. The damn machine was obviously having one of its fits, like the time it insisted that she was in Montreal even though she was definitely in Milwaukee. This particular glitch had taken her so far north of San Francisco, she was almost to Oregon. Nobody lived out in these woods.

The road curved along the mountainside, afternoon sunlight filtering through the ancient redwoods. Everything was quiet out there. Traffic, people, city lights—they were all far, far away. She gripped the steering wheel on her rented Jeep Wrangler, set her jaw, and drove on. If the GPS was unwilling to help, well, then, she was just going to have to find this man on her own. She needed him.

Kyle Weston was the mastermind behind PUMP, Southern California's premier fitness and lifestyle chain.

Celebrities flocked to the Sunset Strip, Santa Barbara, and Laguna Beach locations to get bulked up, slimmed down, made pretty. He was once the top trainer in the nation, and the waiting list to workout with him was over a year long. But then one day, without any warning, he dropped from sight, left L.A. and his franchise behind. He bought some land and sequestered himself way up in the far reaches of the state. Every now and then though, he took on a private client or two, and he was still considered to be one of the best athletic trainers on the planet. Rumor had it that he was behind the careers of many of the elite athletes from around the world. Of course, it was all speculation. He hadn't been seen in public for more than ten years.

Christy followed another wide turn and then blinked hard when a house suddenly appeared on the horizon. She leaned forward, checking it out through the windshield. Even at this distance, she could see that it was huge, a sprawling ranch-style home isolated on acres of land with a giant lake at its back. The owner of that estate obviously had no need or desire for human interaction. It was literally in the middle of nowhere.

"Slight left in one hundred yards," the GPS demanded.

She almost missed the turn she was so startled, her hands shaking as she caught it at the last second, turning onto a freshly paved, deserted road. Tall trees shaded the path, and the air coming in through the car's open windows was markedly cooler. She shivered, her nerves kicking into overdrive, churning up a queasy sickness in her belly as the house drew closer. It had taken weeks and minor miracle to get this appointment. Her entire future rested on what happened next. Finding him was only the beginning of the battle. She still had to convince him that she was worthy. By all accounts, he turned away more people then he accepted, and he was supposedly terrible to be around—terse, taciturn, mercurial. But he got results.

She needed results. In six days, she was going to be competing in the final trial for a spot on the U.S. gymnastics team. And she was going to make that team. Christy Turner was going to be a star at the games and bring home the gold. End of story.

She pulled up the driveway and parked in front of the massive garage about a hundred feet away from the main house. This was it. She reached for the review mirror, angling it down to give herself one last look before getting out of the car. She combed her fingers through her sandy brown hair, then adjusted the scoop neck of her thin cotton top. Unlike a lot of female athletes, she had managed to retain some considerable boobage ... and she made use of them whenever she got the chance. Do me proud, she thought, and gave herself a squeeze. Her own touch sent a wicked thrill through her, and she sat up a little bit straighter. She smiled at herself in the mirror. Much better. She lifted her ass and pulled her muslin skirt up higher on her thigh. This was purely a business meeting, but it didn't hurt to use every advantage. Men had a hard time resisting her, and Kyle

Weston was not going to be an exception.

She exited the car, ready to take on whatever was to come. It was a gorgeous Northern California day, warm but not hot, the air filled with the scent of woods and earth. Birds chirped in the trees, and a rabbit scampered through the woodlands that blanketed the property. Gravel crunched under her feet as she followed the winding path to his front door. *You're here to win.* She exhaled a hard breath, pumping herself up. *You got this.* She gave the front of her shirt an extra tug, offering a slightly better hint of the rounded curve of her breasts.

The door opened just as she stepped onto the porch, and the man standing in the doorway gave her pause. He was nothing like she expected. Kyle Weston had left the public eye when she about ten years old, so she had no real frame of reference for him, but for some reason, she had envisioned him to be old, grizzled, a man well into his sixties with frown lines and a mustache, and hard, leathery skin. The man standing before her wasn't old at all, he'd barely be over thirty-five, if that. And he was pussy-thumping hot. Built like a basketball player, he was tall and muscular, lean, not bulky, and he was all sex—from the top of his golden blond head, right down to his bare feet. But it was the blue eyes that really sold him, the color so intense, they alone were enough to make a girl's panties drop like it was prom night.

A pleasant jolt zapped her cunt as a smile curled her lips. This could be interesting indeed. She held out her hand as she crossed the porch to meet him. "Hello, Mr. Weston.

I'm Christy Turner."

He stood with his arms folded across his chest, his head cocked to the side, looking her up and down. He made no move to take her hand, no move whatsoever, just silently weighed and accessed her. She dropped her hand back to her side. He was not going to faze her. She was here to win. There was no alternative. She gave him her best smile, the one the judges loved, and waited.

Time stretched out. A cool breeze rustled her skirt, the light fabric tickling her thighs. A hawk sliced through the sky above their heads. His gaze was like a physical caress, touching her face, her breasts, her waist, her legs. She tried to be patient, but his scrutiny was making her itchy, horny, lighting a low fire, deep down in her core.

His gaze traveled slowly back up her body, and when their eyes met, the intensity of him pierced her defenses. She was exposed, naked before him, all her dirty thoughts cataloged, cross-referenced, and found disdainfully amusing. Lust blazed through her, sizzling hot. The sheer force of him totally blew her away, and she dropped her gaze, her cheeks burning with a complicated mixture of competitiveness and desire.

Seconds passed. Neither of them moved. Christy stood firm. There was no way she was going home now. She had to work with this man. Without a word, he stepped aside and allowed her to enter.

Her heart raced as she followed him through the doorway into the tastefully appointed living room. The dark furniture, exposed beams, and wood accents were rustic, masculine, and perfectly suited to the man before her. Her gaze touched on his broad shoulders, the curve of his spine, his high, firm ass. She wanted him, and it wasn't hard to imagine what his cock might taste like. After she got what she needed from him, she was definitely going to fuck him.

They took a right and entered his office, a wide open space featuring more dark wood and a breathtaking view of the expanse of nature around them. Mountains rose in the distance, a ragged line in the never-ending stretch of blue sky. She tore her eyes from the bay windows and took in the mahogany desk, the bookshelves lining the walls, the various framed certificates and diplomas. There was only one chair in the room, an executive leather recliner back behind the desk.

He sat down, and it seemed that she had no choice but to remain standing. Fine with her. His little set-ups and antics weren't going to intimidate her. She stood before him with her hands clasped against the small of her back.

He studied her again, another slow, detailed appraisal, then leaned forward, and steepled his fingers under his chin. "Why did you come here?"

His voice was deep, meditative, the question quiet and reflective. She met his gaze for an instant before her eyes skipped away. "They say you're the best. I only work with the best."

He nodded slowly. "You're old for a competitive gymnast."

Her upper lip curled in disdain. "I'm twenty. In perfect shape. And I have more experience and drive than any of those virgin harpies."

Was there a hint of a smile on his full lips? Did those blue eyes linger over her breasts, the curve of her waist? She thought so. Gymnastics training might not be the only skills that needed to be perfected over their time together. She had some other muscle groups that could use a nice, hard workout as well.

His gaze moved down her body to focus on her legs. "What about the injury that kept you out of the last games? Is that an issue? Many athletes don't ever fully recover from severe tears."

She swallowed back the bile that rose in her throat as the memory of the day her tendon snapped assaulted her, the sickening pop in her knee, and then the pain, mingled with embarrassment and fury. Two seconds, one bad landing, and *poof*—her dreams were over. So sorry, see you in four years, she was told, and she was replaced by a girl who hadn't had the skill to qualify in the first place. Well, four years had passed. It was time for her to claim the spot that was rightfully hers. "I'm better than ever."

His face was impassive, neither impressed nor distressed by her bravado. "I've seen the tapes. Your vault was decent, your beam work was adequate though lackluster, but it was the floor exercise where you lost the most points. Why is that?"

Her skin prickled and rage made her blood run hot.

She was the ultimate comeback, the feel-good story of the games, the pretty young woman who overcame grievous injury to win the gold. Everything was in her favor. Maybe her routine was a tad shaky, but that was even more reason for the judges to be a bit lenient with her. She had worked harder than any of those other girls to be on that mat. She should have scored higher. "The judges were obviously having a bad day."

He raised a single eyebrow. "You would have to put out a phenomenal effort to make the team at this point." He leaned forward, toward her, his hands flat on the desk. "Are you willing to do that?"

She scoffed. She was there wasn't she? "Of course."

The leather creaked as he sat back in the chair. "I don't think you are."

"What?" She was so flabbergasted her mouth hung open. "Why not?"

"Because you don't have what it takes. We've only just met, and I already know that you're a princess. Arrogant. Entitled." He rose from the chair and stood toe to toe with her. He was huge, almost a foot-and-a-half taller than she was, and he dominated the entire room. He deliberately dropped his gaze to her cleavage. "Being fuckable does not make you a good gymnast." He bent down a little farther into her space. "Discipline makes you a good gymnast. The strength and drive to push further, work harder, go to the very ends of your endurance, and *still do better*." He dropped his voice, held her gaze. "You are nowhere near as good as you think you are. But you could be. You could be the absolute best and have the entire world know it." He shook his head. "But I don't think you're willing to go to the lengths you need to in order to get what you want. Not even for all that glory."

Glory was the only thing she had ever wanted. It was her destiny. He had no idea what she was capable of. She leaned into him, bared her teeth. "I am the best fucking gymnast you will ever know."

Time stretched out between them once again. Their eyes clashed, a silent battle of wills. She would not look away this time. Not for anything.

"Y-scale," he commanded.

Responding to such a directive was an innate response, ingrained into her very being by decades of coaching. She didn't even think, immediately lifting her left leg into the air, supporting her ankle in her left hand, and extending her right hand out and up, her body creating a standing Y shape. Her cold, tense muscles weren't prepared for the sudden stretch, however, and she failed to reach the perfect form.

He circled around her, taking his time to look her over. He stopped behind her, so close his body heat touched her skin. She breathed him in, the clean scent of soap and *Sequoia Blue*, and desire raced through her veins. Placing one hand on her hip, he ran the other up the back of her calf, a light caress that went from her knee to her ankle. He crouched to speak softly and directly into her ear. "You're about forty degrees off center."

She fought back the shivers that wanted to cascade along her nerve endings and concentrated on elongating her muscles, maneuvering them in into the proper position. His breath on the back of her neck made her cheeks hot, but it was the challenge in his voice that really got her blood pumping.

"Higher," he said, and tapped the back of her thigh.

His grip tightened on her hip as she repositioned herself, helping to hold her steady. "Very nice," he said, even closer. The scrape of his stubble against her cheek sent heat spiraling down to her pussy. "Now stand a little taller."

She did as she was told, her muscles finally warming up enough to be malleable. She straightened her spine and lifted her chin. On her raised leg, he traced a path from her calf, to her knee, then down the long, smooth line of her hamstring. Her skin tingled from his touch, and her breath caught when he reached the edge of her panties. He fingered the lace border, following the crease flesh where her thigh met her torso. Arousal moistened her inner folds, and she trembled.

"Concentrate," he snapped.

She gasped when he spanked her pussy, the sudden sting sharp and hot. She wanted to mold herself to his body and writhe against him, but she closed her eyes instead, breathed out, and found her balance. Pretty soon, she was going to turn around, rip off his clothes, throw him on the floor, and fuck him hard. That one thought kept her upright.

"Good." He ran fingers back up her hamstring.

"Now bring your leg higher."

She planted her foot on the ground, and stretched her leg up farther, inching it closer to the top of her head. The edge of fatigue was creeping in, her muscles starting to ache. She'd never held a y-scale for this long before, never stretched this far in her life. She wasn't sure how much longer she could maintain it.

"Hold it." His fingers moved down her calf again, fondling the hard muscle, then caressed the back of her knee before gilding along her inner thigh. She clenched her teeth when he stroked the length of her slit, tickling her folds over the thin, lacy material of her panties. "Just like that," he murmured while he tormented her.

She was on fire, her pussy throbbing, her muscles nearly at the end of their strength. Every light caress made her wetter, her juices saturating her underwear. She battled through the discomfort, the blinding arousal, struggling to remain upright.

"Whatever happens— *Do not come.*" He reached beneath her skirt and ripped open the crotch of her panties.

Cool air touched her hot folds, and she whimpered, a plea, a denial, something beyond words. The pain had become perversely erotic, excruciating and lascivious. She moaned when he touched her swollen clit, immediately bringing her hips up to meet his finger.

"Hold. The. Form." He punctuated each word with a brutal slap to her bare, vulnerable pussy.

The punishing jolt blasted along her nerve endings.

She wanted to squirm, she wanted to escape, she wanted the fierce sting to go on forever and forever. Every successive spank made her wetter, even as her muscles screamed to relax. She forced her body back into a perfect Y, and the pain stopped, but only to be replaced with a new kind of torture when his finger returned to her clit. Her pussy flooded with liquid heat, ready to orgasm. Don't come? Was he insane? How was she not going to come? One more stroke, and it was all going to be over.

His manipulations ceased, and he cupped her mound. His breath was harsh in her ear, the rise and fall of his chest heavy against her back. She hoped that he was hard, that his cock was straining against his jeans, aching to fill her, needing to fuck·her as much as she wanted to fuck him.

"One goal," he whispered to her. "Your only thoughts should be on winning. About presenting the perfect form. You want to be the best? There's only one way to do that. Total commitment." His grip tightened on her hip, and he ran his slick fingertips up the back of her thigh. "Now raise your leg higher."

Everything in her screamed that she could not do it, that there was no higher, that she was at every limit she could ever possibly endure, but his fingers returned to her clit and she reached deep into herself, deep down into the very core of her stubborn, competitive will, and raised her leg higher.

"That's very good," he purred.

Her body burned to come, burned to relax. Her muscles strained, her pussy ached. She wanted to collapse.

She wanted to ride his cock like a wild cowgirl. It was too much. She did not want to hold back any longer, not when the reward was so very sweet.

His middle finger eased down her slit and tapped her entrance. Her pussy contracted, wanting to draw him in. He pushed inside and her head fell back against his shoulder. Liquid coated his hand as he pushed deeper, and when his finger curled, she was done. She had maintained the position longer than any gymnast would ever be asked to hold it, she'd stood still while he spanked her, while he tormented her, while he made her wet and needy and hot. But this was too much. Too good. She'd fight later. For now, she was going to be satisfied. She let herself go, exploding with a cry, her cunt drenching his fingers. He worked her hard as wave after wave rocked her, stroking her orgasm to insane heights until she was literally screaming for mercy, for him to stop, for it to never end.

And then he pulled away. Without his support, she dropped to the floor, a wretched pile of mush. Her pussy thrummed, her legs shook, her whole body was flushed. The aftershocks quaked through her as she lay there, sprawled at his feet.

He stood over her for a long moment before hunkering down beside her. "You have no discipline."

And that was it. He rose to his feet and turned toward the exit. Once he crossed that threshold, it was all over. She slammed her fist against the hardwood floor. She was not going to let him walk out of there, leave her alone and defeated, forced to vacate his house with her head hanging and her tail between her legs. That was not the way this story was going to end. She gritted her teeth and dragged herself to her feet. She could feel him pause, sense his attention. Tenacity had to count for something. Everyone fell once in a while. It was how you got up that made you a woman. She had to believe that was true or everything was lost. Her muscles screamed in protest, but she raised her leg, and despite the pain, the fatigue, the erotic pulse vibrating in her pussy, assumed the position once more.

Everything was still in the office, the sound of her own breathing loud in her ears. Her body ached, but she held her ground by sheer force of will. She was not going to fail. Not today. Not ever. What felt like hours passed. The floor creaked as his weight shifted. Her heart jackhammered. This was it.

"You'll be staying in the guest bedroom, down the hallway, the second door on the right. I expect you to be in the basement gym at five a.m." He paused. "I'll have my housekeeper bring dinner to your room at seven. Perhaps you should spend the night mediating on what you truly want. There is only one way to be a champion."

She stood there, exhausted but triumphant, and listened to the sound of his footsteps grow faint as he walked away.

Chapter Two

Christy paced the room for the hundredth time. Dark blue walls, bookshelves, queen-size bed, wood dresser, sliding glass doors, and then back around again. There was nothing else to do. No TV, no internet. She'd already eaten dinner, and she wasn't hungry for any more food. There were books, but she'd never been much of a reader, and she was far too keyed up sit still anyway.

She contemplated taking another shower, but dismissed the idea. It hadn't worked the first time, and she doubted the results would be any different now. After her "interview," she'd taken a hot shower to try to soothe her poor, overworked muscles. She might as well have taken a cold one for the good it did. Her muscles might have been tired, but her pussy was wide awake and begging for more attention. The torment of his clever fingers was fresh in her mind, and she'd touched herself, reliving the way he'd messaged her clit, the long, deep stroke that ended it all. But, no matter how hard she concentrated, she couldn't make herself come. She'd rubbed herself raw and only achieved frustration. The problem was, she needed more than her own fingers and the memories of his touch.

She spun on her heel and walked back up the length of the room. He told her to meditate on what she wanted. Well, she wanted him. Right now. Her pussy was already slick and ready for him to slide all the way inside her, to fill her up with his tongue, his fingers, his cock. How she'd love to climb her way up that toned body and ride him until he was the one moaning and writhing. Dig her fingernails into his fine ass and use him until she was spent, fucked dry. And then maybe ride him some more.

She went for the door, but stopped as her fingers closed around the knob. It was that attitude that landed her ass on the floor. She'd fuck him—that was totally going to happen—but now was not the time. If she went to him tonight, he'd send her home for sure, and she needed his help.

She turned away from the temptation and crossed the room to look out the sliding glass doors. The lake glimmered in the moonlight, beautiful and serene. She hadn't taken a nighttime run in a long time, not since she left her parents' ranch in New Mexico for the big city and fame, and the notion seemed almost romantic in its perfection. Even more importantly, it would be a productive way to burn off some of her restlessness.

She threw on some shorts, sneakers, a sweatshirt, and slipped out of the bedroom. The back patio was lit by subtle track lighting, creating a soft, warm glow around the house. She set off along the path around the lake, passing trees and shrubs and plants that she had no names for. The feel of dirt and dried twigs crunching beneath her feet was comforting. The air held a woodsy, clean scent, and the moon and stars gave the world a silvery luster. She'd forgotten how big the sky could be, how many stars there were out there when the night was not muted by city lights.

Her breathing steadied as she found her pace, falling into a nice, smooth jog. Her mind wandered, touching on little things—she needed to pay her phone bill when she got back, she should arrange for a better suite in the hotel she would be staying at in Atlanta for the trials, and then finally settled on Kyle Weston and his piercing blue gaze. She smiled to herself as a whole different kind of warmth heated her muscles. Dear God, but he was hot. Infuriating, but downright fucking sexy. He played her hard; and she, as much as she hated to admit it, she had liked it. Hell, *loved* it. She already felt more competitive than she had in years. That fire was back, alive again in her blood, combating the desperation that ruled over her ever since the trials. It had been a long time since anyone had challenged her, since she'd had any reason to fight. It felt good to be taken to the edge again. It felt right.

And then, when he made her great, when he took her to the level where she needed to be, then she would sink her hands into his short, blond hair and guide his mouth down to where she wanted him to be.

A wolf howled in the distance, and Christy blew out a deliberately hard breath. She wiped the sheen of sweat off her forehead with the back of her forearm and rubbed her eyes to dispel the images. She needed to get sex off the brain. Thinking about him was not relieving any of her tension. It was only making it worse.

All she ever wanted was to be a world-famous gymnast. Not a good a gymnast, not even a great one—the *best*. She knew at age six when she entered her first class that it was what she wanted to do with the rest of her life, to be able to move her body gracefully, be beautiful and strong. The moment she won her first competition and got that heady taste of victory, she was hooked. Nothing in life felt as good as competing hard and winning.

Making the team again should have been a non-issue, but the unthinkable had occurred. She had nearly failed. That had never happened to her before. It was unacceptable, and she was afraid. For the first time in her life, she might not succeed. Her competition was younger, more vibrant, and though she'd never admit it out loud, some of her confidence had snapped right along with her tendon. She was still good, but there was a whisper in the back of her mind now that had never been there before, the worry that it could happen again. And maybe that had made her a little complacent, a little soft. Maybe she hadn't been pushing herself as hard she should have, maybe she had been giving in to her more selfish needs, allowing herself a little too much "comfort."

Whatever the reasons, all that had to end. Because what if she didn't make the team? A terrifying thought, but one that she had to seriously consider. Where did washed-up gymnasts go? Was there some kind of gymnastic equivalent of the Ice Capades out there? Could she really spend the rest of her life on the road, wearing garish face paint and spangly suits?

No. Just—*no*. That could not be allowed to happen. It was not too late. She was going to succeed, and Kyle Weston was going to help her do it.

She rounded the curve of the lake leading back to the house and light from the master bedroom caught her eye. The curtains were drawn back from the sliding glass doors, but the room was dim, shadows obscuring most of her view. She drew closer and movement in the depths of the room made her pause. Some instinctual part of her brain demanded that she hide, and she dropped off the path to crouch in the shrubbery.

Nothing stirred in the darkness, but something was going to happen. It was like electricity in the air. A few seconds passed, then a minute, and then he came into view. She gasped, but pressed her hands over her mouth to muffle the sound. He was stark naked and gorgeously backlit by the low light in the room. His body was perfect, sculpted and lean, and the shadows played along the curves and contours of his muscles. She slowly worked her gaze over every inch of him, eating up the sight—broad chest, wide shoulders tapering down to a narrow waist, six-pack abs, powerful thighs. And his cock, semi-hard and nestled in patch of dark blond hair.

He looked out into the night, at the sky, the lake, the woods, and finally, her. The threat of discovery pinned her to the ground and she held her breath. She tried to calm her thundering pulse with the knowledge that she was good distance away from the house. He probably couldn't see her. Yet it seemed like his eyes lingered over the spot where she hid, located her in the darkness, and then moved on. It was foolish in the extreme, but she crawled backward, deeper into the foliage nonetheless.

He stood there for an eternity, naked and stunning, and then he started stroking his cock.

Christy gulped, her pussy instantly wet. Her eyes followed his hand as it glided over the shaft. His dick grew in his fist, big and succulent and fat, and she licked her lips when he gave the head a squeeze.

His head tilted back as he found a rhythm, stroking himself a little faster. His Adam's apple bounced in his throat when he swallowed. She hoped the images playing out behind his closed eyes included her and featured multiple scenarios of bending her over his desk and giving her every inch of that luscious cock. She'd spread her legs for him anytime, as long as he promised to give it to her hard and not stop until she was fully sated.

"Oh, yesss …" she breathed out. She was down on all fours, not the position she liked to be in when she touched herself, but she didn't let that deter her from slipping her hand under the waistband of her shorts and diving into her panties. Her middle finger touched her clit, and the electric thrill made her nipples hard. She shivered as she moved her hand lower, then groaned in total satisfaction when she slid her finger deep into her wet cunt.

He slapped the glass door, and she jumped, the sound clear and sharp even over the distance. His hand pressed against the glass, his fingers splayed as he braced himself. The tendons stood out in his neck as he stroked faster, pumping his hips into his fist. She knew that he was close, and she panted, working hard to catch up with him. She found her g-spot and pressed. Her hips bucked from the white-hot surge of pleasure and a low moan escaped her parted lips.

The large muscles in his thighs tensed just as a warm flush spread over her body. She stroked herself faster, rocking on her knees to get where she needed to be. She looked up just in time to see the cum shoot from his cock, hit the glass, his stomach, drip down over his knuckles. It was the hottest thing she'd ever witnessed, and it took her right over the edge. Her muscles went stiff as the orgasm shook her, rattling her brains and making her whole body buzz.

She pressed her forehead to the ground to catch her breath, and when she was able to lift her head again, she swore their eyes met across the distance. It was a punch in the gut that lasted a single heartbeat, so short, it had to be imaginary. She watched him turn away from the window, the shadows heightening the deep dimples over his fine ass before he moved out of sight, leaving her alone in the dark.

◇◇◇◇

Five a.m. came early, but Christy was up and ready

with ten minutes to spare. She found the basement door easily enough and walked down the short staircase. She wasn't sure what she expected, but it certainly wasn't the gleaming expanse before her. State of the art equipment lined the mirrored walls—all sorts of weights and machines on the mat while ropes and rings hung from the ceiling. It was an athlete's wet dream come true, a totally custom gym that was probably larger than the house above it. And there, right in the center of it all, was a regulation-sized floor mat.

It took her minute to notice that he was already there, leaning back against the pommel horse, looking sexy in basketball shorts, a gray T-shirt, and bare feet. That shirt pulled tight over the muscles in his chest, and she was instantly reminded of how he looked naked, how defined that torso really was. He twirled a thick black cane around with his thumb and wrist, the sliver handle flashing as it slowly rotated in his hand.

She crossed the mat to stand before him, but she couldn't quite meet his gaze. Her eyes wandered to the rowing machine, the weight benches. Did he know? There was no way he could know. Her gaze flicked to his crotch and then quickly away. No, she couldn't let her mind go there, no matter how tempting the thought.

"Start with your usual warm up exercises." He pointed the tip of the cane at her, waved it over her body. "And get rid of that thing you're wearing. I need to see your muscles working."

She looked down at her sleeveless workout leotard,

confusion knitting her brows. "You want me naked?"

He frowned. "Am I speaking a language that you don't understand?"

She snapped back to attention. "No."

"Then do it." He slapped the stick against his palm. "Let's go!"

She stripped as quickly as she could and began her routine of stretches, lifts, splits, cardio. He sat on top of the pommel horse, watching her closely, holding the cane between his thighs. She could feel his gaze on her through every leap, every stretch, but if he was moved at all by the sight of her naked body bending and twisting, he showed no sign.

Her body warmed to the familiar exercise, and she felt good, confident and loose. His attention stimulated the ever-present lust bubbling deep down in her core, and she added little flourishes to the routine for his benefit, an extra little bounce here, a longer wiggle there, and she ended it all with a high kick that gave him a flashing peek at her pussy.

He raised an eyebrow at her, and though he appeared mostly unimpressed, she definitely noticed a faint smile on his lips. He picked up the remote control resting beside him atop the horse, and her signature music came on—the jazzy, bebop composition that accompanied her floor exercise. "All right," he said. "Show me your floor routine."

She started off strong with a double layout. Her landing was solid, and she smiled as she went right into her standing split. She met his eyes when she lifted her leg, the position allowing him a full, unrestricted view of her sex. She held the split slightly longer than necessary and then rolled into a tumble that gave him a great view of her ass. Another split, another chance to show him everything from cleft to clit. Moisture tickled her inner folds, her body heating in a million different ways. Her gaze danced over him, the memory of his cock swelling in his fist inspiring a delicious throb deep in her cunt. Goose bumps pricked her skin. If he fucked her half as hard as he'd jerk himself off she'd be screaming for—

"STOP!"

The music cut out and Christy froze, her arms raised artfully in the air. Her eyes went wide as he stormed across the mat toward her.

"What the hell are you doing?"

"Wha—?" A thought didn't have time to form in her head. He brought the cane down on her ass, one swift move that sliced the air behind her back and delivered a stinging bite to her buttocks.

"What. Was. That?" He enunciated each word carefully. "I don't know what you were thinking about, but it certainly wasn't your routine."

She stared at the hollow of this throat, heat radiating out across her butt cheeks. The bulk of the cane rested just below her ass, right at the top of her thighs. The weight of it sent chills of fear and ghastly anticipation rolling down her spine.

He leaned down, his lips close to her ear. "What was

going through your mind when you made a tragedy of that beautiful routine?"

"I ... ah ... wasn't really ..." What could she say? Her mind was blank. There was only the cane, the heat of his body, his breath on her throat.

He rolled the stick over her ass, the wood cool against her hot skin. "Think carefully before you answer."

"Your cock," she blurted out. "I was thinking about your cock."

He brought the silver handle under her chin, forcing her head up. "That's correct. You were more concerned about showing me your pussy, than properly executing your moves."

She bowed her head. There was nothing to say. He was right. And it chafed.

"I told you yesterday to think about what discipline means to you, what you hoped to get out of our training." He followed her eyes, refusing to allow her to look away. "Did you spend last night doing that?"

She considering lying, but decided against it. "No."

"No, you did not." He ran the handle of the cane along the line of her jaw. "Did you like watching me jerk off?" She tasted the silver when it touched her lips, tracing the seam of her mouth. "Did you like coming with me?"

The mortification of being caught twined with the thrill, and her pussy flooded with raw, liquid heat. The tension between them made the air thick, difficult to breathe. Her heart raced, and every cell in her body tingled.

"We can fuck right now if that's what you want." He dipped his head, and his breath touched her lips, warm and minty. His gaze flicked to her mouth. "I can send you home a very satisfied woman."

"No," she whispered, her voice cracking. She wanted him so bad. But she wanted his help more. "I want to stay."

He looked deep into her eyes. "Discipline. Intention. Those are the keys to your success." He lifted the cane, glanced at it, then back to her. "What are your intentions?"

She straightened her spine. "To be the best."

"Then act like it."

She bit down on the inside of her cheek as the cane came down on her ass. She tried not to cry out, but it was impossible after the first few blows, the pain too sweet and terrible to handle. Tears came, but she stood still and took the punishment. If she wanted all that he had to offer, then she had to pay the price. The fifth blow landed and then he stopped. He put a hand on her shoulder and leaned down into her space.

"Look at me," he commanded. She met his gaze. "Do it right."

He believed in her, in her ability, there was no question of that in his gaze. His conviction demanded that she believe in herself as well, that she live up to her potential, and be as good as she actually was.

She wiped her face and crossed the mat to take her position at the starting point. When the music came on again, she concentrated on executing the moves, turning her body to highlight the most appealing form, to gain the most points from the judges. Her ass burned, a constant reminder of her purpose. Her toes pointed, her muscles flexed, and she worked harder than ever before, harder even than at the tryout. She worked to show him that she could, to prove that his faith was not unwarranted. She worked to show herself that she could, that she was still the best, and she worked for the pure joy of it, for the love of dance and movement. When she reached the end of the routine, she was breathless and exhilarated, her body flushed with heat and success. She executed the final move and waited for some well-earned praise.

"Slightly better," he said, from across the mat. "But nowhere near where we need to be at this late date."

"What?" she asked, her mouth slightly agape. "'Slightly better'? That's it?" She put her hands on her hips. "I think that was pretty damn awesome."

He smiled, but there was nothing comforting about it. "I will let you know when you reach 'pretty damn awesome'. For now, however, our work continues." He twirled the cane in his fingers. "I think we need to break down the routine piece by piece, focus on the individual components, and isolate your weaknesses from there." He looked her over again and nodded once. "Begin."

She blinked, too surprised to argue, and before she knew it, he was guiding her through each separate skill, analyzing it, and then perfecting it. He showed her how to increase the difficulty level of her back handspring, which would definitely earn her a lot more points from the judges, and instructed her in a better way to land after her dive cartwheel. It was grinding, tedious work, but every suggestion, every adjustment made her routine stronger.

When he finally called it a day, she was panting, sweaty, wrung out, but better than ever. Her routine was tighter now, she knew it in her heart. He was a tremendous coach, the best she had ever worked with.

"You did well," he said, and there was a new kind of twinkle in his eye, one she liked a whole lot. "Would you like a reward?"

A smile curved her lips, a lick of fire heating her core. "What kind of reward?"

He shook his head, feigning disappointment. "I asked you a simple question, Christy. Would you like a reward or not?"

She smiled a little wider. Something wicked was happening here. "Yes, I would like a reward."

"Come over here."

He held her gaze as she crossed the mat, then looked pointedly at the ground at his feet. She got the message and went to her knees before him. Ferocious triumph raced through her veins. She was finally going to get a piece of his cock. Oh, yes, indeed. She looked at the bulge in his shorts and then up into his eyes.

He reached down, cupped her breast in his palm, and rolled her nipple between his thumb and forefinger. It hardened instantly in his fingers, and when he tugged, the sharp pain collided with the intense pleasure. "Go on," he said. "Take it out."

She curled her hands around the waistband of his shorts and pulled them down. He stepped out of them and kicked them aside. His cock was even more impressive up close, and a delightful shiver ran over her. She licked her lips, leaned forward, and gave the head a soft, wet kiss. She felt the vibrations of his moan right down in the very core of her pussy. Holding his gaze, she pushed up his T-shirt and licked his stomach, tracing the line down the center of his abs, dragging her tongue over the length of his treasure trail, to the base of his cock. He gasped when she delivered wet butterfly kisses along his shaft. He cupped the back of her head, and she obeyed the silent direction, taking him into her mouth.

"Good girl," he breathed out. "Now, suck."

His hips began to move, a deliberate, rhythmic thrust. The taste of him exploded on her tongue, and she sat up a little higher to taste more of him. She wanted him to fuck her pussy just like he was fucking her mouth, slow and steady and deep. She reached between her legs to finger her clit, moaning around his cock as she moistened her cunt for him.

The cane snapped down on her ass, and she cried out, startled by the sudden sting and agonizing heat. He pressed the tip of the cane against her shoulder and pushed her away. "Did I tell you to do that?"

She sat back on her heels, looking up at him, her pussy on fire. He was speaking, but the words weren't making any sense. She wanted to suck, fuck, not talk. "What?"

He tapped the cane against her ass, not hard, but enough to reignite the tenderness. "What did I tell you to do?"

She tried to focus. What was the last thing he'd said? "Suck?"

"That's right," he said. "Did I tell you to do anything else?"

She shook her head. No, there hadn't been any words after that one.

"Then follow the directions." He gripped the base of his cock and bought the head to her lips. "Open your mouth." She did as she was told and he slid inside. He held the cane against her spine, the wood was cold and smooth against her back. He took a fistful of her hair in his other hand and plunged deep into her mouth.

She held on as best she could, her hands on his thighs as he pounded her throat. He grunted, fucking her mouth for his own pleasure. A few hard thrusts, and his grip tightened in her hair. The next moment, he was exploding down her throat, and she struggled to swallow every drop of his cum.

When he was finally spent, he pulled back with a sigh. She wiggled, her pussy wet and heavy and ready for her turn to come. Would he fuck her on her knees? From behind? Would he pump into her again and again, until she was overfilled with every inch of his fat cock? Oh, yeah. She wanted all of that. Immediately.

He touched her bottom lip gently, then ran his thumb

up over her cheek. "Did you like that?"

"Yes," she said, bouncing with excitement.

"Good," he said, and then stepped back, out of her reach. "Spend the rest of the afternoon working on those *jetés en tournant*. They're sloppy. And I want you to do that double tuck with your hands on your shins, not on the back of your thighs. You did the routine well, but you're obviously still undecided about what you truly want. Let me help you make that decision. You are forbidden from touching yourself until I give you express permission otherwise." He held up his index finger. "One goal, Christy. No distractions. You can't win if you're not committed. Do we understand one another?"

Her pussy was throbbing. She *needed* to come. But the look on his face made any protests die in her mouth. Did she even want to take on this test? Was it worth it? She bit back the gnawing need and clenched her fists. Priorities. She looked up into his eyes. "Yes, I understand."

He nodded once and left the gym.

Chapter Three

Days passed. Nights came and went. They did drills. Cardio. Beam work. Hours upon hours on the uneven bars. Her vault dismount was so outrageous, it would take the gold all on its own. Every aspect of her game improved.

But it was torture. He made sure that it was. She'd showed up the first morning and knew she was in trouble the minute she saw his smile. All day long he tormented her with blatant gropes and subtle caresses, spankings, and light taps of the cane. She barely made it through the entire workout, and the only thing that held her back was the sadistic twinkle in his eyes and her refusal to give him any satisfaction.

She survived the day, but it was for the wrong reason, she reflected in her bed that night. She had not begged and pulled strings, called in favors and made promises, to travel halfway across the country just to fuck Kyle Weston. It would have been nice, and she'd still love the chance, but he made her choose. The decision wasn't all that difficult once she finally accepted there was no way to have both. She went to sleep horny, but at peace with herself.

The next morning was better. He still physically seduced her in grand and raunchy ways, but now that her focus had shifted, she found that his distractions weren't really all that distracting. She was able to concentrate on his words rather than just his roaming hands. And listening to him speak, she started to believe in his message, in his faith in her endurance and beauty and power. As they worked, the whisper of fear began to fade from her mind, and for the first time since her injury, she felt totally free on the mat again, confident and strong. She still went to bed with a wet and needy pussy, but it didn't matter so much anymore.

And then the last day arrived. The end of it all.

He was waiting for her in the gym as usual, sitting atop his pommel horse. "Since you're leaving tomorrow and this will be the last time we work together, I'm going to give you a choice." He looked her over, that penetrating gaze that always got her a little bit wet. "Would you like to train or would you like to come?"

Very tempting, but she shook her head. "I want to train."

"Are you sure?"

She raised her eyebrows. There was something definitely going on here. "Yes, I'm sure."

He leapt off the horse, twirling the cane as he circled around her. "I admire your determination."

She laughed. "No, you don't."

"Maybe," he said and smiled. It was the first real smile she'd seen on his lips since she arrived. He was such a ridiculously gorgeous man, and that smile made her insides hum. "We'll see how today goes."

She felt more naked before him today than ever before, his gaze dirty, indecent, and totally hot, but she also detected some admiration there, and her heart filled with pride.

"You've done well," he said, and leaned on the cane. "We've worked hard these last few days and your muscles need a rest before you compete in the final trial. We're going to end our work with some inversion therapy."

She waited. No way was it going to be that easy. He put the cane aside and escorted her to the far corner of the gym to a custom inversion therapy table. A long rectangular metal frame rested in a triangular stand, the stand allowing the frame to pivot through 180 degrees of movement. Unlike normal therapy tables, this one had a long bar across the bottom of the frame with gravity boots affixed to the corners and wrist restraints attached to the top of the board.

He helped her onto the device and locked her feet and wrists into the waiting cuffs. Her whole body was stretched out on the table, her legs wide apart, her wrists locked together above her head. Then, he gently tipped the frame 180 degrees so that she was upside down. She exhaled into the stretch, releasing the tension in her back, calves, thighs, shoulders. It was incredible, and she reached for the floor, her fingertips brushing against the mat, moaning in total ecstasy as she worked out all the kinks out of her spine.

"Nice?" he asked, watching the clock on the wall. Being upside down for too long could be dangerous.

She closed her eyes, safe in his care. "Really, really

good."

He ran his finger along the outside curve of her foot. "Do you feel prepared?"

"I do," she said. "I get it now. No distractions." She smiled, but it was a shame. He would have been a wonderful distraction. But, she made her decision, and it was the right one. "I was so caught up in other things—the injury, the hype of a comeback, my public persona—I forgot what was important." She opened her eyes and looked up at him. Even upside down, he was pussy-pulsing sexy. "I won't forget again."

He ran his fingers along her shin, stopping at her knee. "I didn't think you'd make it, honestly."

"Oh no?" Her skin tingled as his hand moved along her thigh.

"No, I thought you'd break by the second night, sneak into my bedroom, be waiting naked under my covers." He caressed her stomach, her ribs, cupped her breast. "I almost hoped you would."

She had thought about it, almost that exact scenario. "Why?" she asked, teasing him. "Do you want to fuck me that badly?"

"Well," he said, dragging out the word as he slowly brought her back up to a horizontal position. "Mostly I wanted a really good reason to beat your ass red."

She laughed. "Like that ever stopped you."

He shook his head. "That's not true."

She conceded with a grunt. He was right, everything

he did had a specific purpose. And however uncomfortable it may have been, it was all to her advantage. Still, she didn't have to like it or admit it out loud.

He smiled. He knew. He ducked beneath the frame and her to stand between her open thighs. He held on to her cuffed wrists and then gently rubbed her forearms, her biceps and triceps, her deltoid and pectorals, her upper abs. "You have a magnificent body."

"Thanks," she said, enjoying the deep massage, his firm, but tender touch.

He ran his thumb from her navel down to her clit, and pressed the sensitive nub hard. "And a very wet pussy."

She sighed as he stroked her, allowing her arousal to heat her body from the inside out.

His thumb moved in a tiny circle that made her toes curl uncontrollably. "How many times did you touch yourself without my permission?"

"Not once." And she was glad she was able to say that with pride and no regrets.

"Why not?" He dipped his thumb into her pussy, just enough to tease, then pulled it out.

She breathed out a shaky breath. He knew just how to make her throb. "Because I made my decision."

"And what was that?" He slipped his index finger all the way inside her and brought his thumb to her clit.

She couldn't control the shudder that ran over her, but that didn't mean she was going to give in. She smiled and met his gaze. "To follow directions and have some discipline."

He added his middle finger. "You sure about that?"

Her hips jerked when those long fingers curled inside her. She fought back the heat and managed to maintain her smile. "Yup."

He lifted off his T-shirt, dropped his shorts. Her heart raced and her internal temperature rocketed up a thousand degrees. She'd wanted that cock for so very long, and her eyes fixed on it, on the deliberate stroke of his hand as he made himself harder. He stepped forward, pressing the head against her opening. "Shall we find out?"

Animal lust drenched her cunt, and the competitiveness in her soul roared to life. "Oh, yeah."

He breathed out as he slid inside her. Her pussy closed around him, squeezing him tight. He pushed deeper, in all the way to the hilt. She clamped down on him, and was fiercely pleased when he groaned. He gave her an evil grin and set a slow, steady pace, stroking over every inch of her hungry, needy pussy. The embers that had been burning all week in her core exploded into a wildfire. She ached for release, but she was in total control.

She lifted her hips to meet him thrust for thrust. She wanted to lick him, taste his flesh, sink her teeth into his hard muscles and ride him hard, but she was bound tight. The wrist restraints cut into her skin as she struggled to touch him. She moaned in frustration fueled by desire, and thrashed against the shackles, but there was no give. All she could do was grip him with her pussy muscles, milk his cock with every bit of strength she had.

"Oh, fuck," he breathed out. "You love my cock, don't you?"

It was her turn to grin. "It's all right."

He pulled back, almost all the way out and then plunged back in again. Her eyes rolled back in her head as he filled her deeper than she ever imagined possible. He tormented her clit with his thumbnail, the pleasure so intense it was excruciating. She cried out, unable to help herself.

"Okay," she said, panting through every thrust. "I love your cock!"

He laughed and picked up his pace, plunging into her hard, fucking her deep. This new rhythm was mind-bendingly good, and she had to focus all her will on not coming, on not giving in, but still enjoying every bit of the ride.

He reached back, unhooked her right ankle, and in one, fluid motion brought her leg up, pinning her knee to her shoulder. He sank in deeper and she groaned, the world threatening to shatter behind her eyes. But she refused to come. She clenched her teeth and freed her leg from his grasp to wrap it around his waist. Her heel dug into his ass, and her back arched up off the board as she rocked her hips against his as hard as she could. He captured her leg again, brought her ankle up by her ear. She moaned, her head falling back against the board as he filled her to her deepest depths, over and over.

He leaned down, his breath hot on her skin. "Do you want to come now?"

"Yes." She couldn't deny it. She wanted it so much.

"Ask me."

She looked into his eyes, squeezed his cock deep within her. "Please, let me come."

"And if I said no?"

Yes, she wanted to come. Yes, she wanted to ride out every single ounce of pleasure he owed her. But she could wait because she didn't need to take the quick and easy way anymore. She could earn her true reward. She had the strength, the discipline, and the stamina. And when he said yes, because she knew he eventually would, she was going to take every last bit of satisfaction she could from him. She met his eyes and smiled. "I can wait."

He smiled back, his pounding thrusts rocking her body. Their rhythm fell into perfect sync, the sounds of their breathing, the slap of their bodies meeting and parting filled the gym. He held her gaze and pressed his thumb to her clit. "Come hard."

Her whole body trembled as she used all of her strength to ride out the release she had so richly earned. Her toes curled, her fingers dug into the restraints as she screamed out the orgasm that set every nerve ending in her body aflame, detonating a nuclear a chain reaction of pleasure.

He thrust harder, every pummeling stroke taking her higher as he strove for his own release. A shudder ran over him, and he pulled out suddenly, grunting as he shot his load on her stomach and breasts. He jerked himself off until every drop had landed on her skin, then he fell forward, gripping the metal frame to brace himself as he loomed over her. He touched her face, a light caress over her cheekbone. "Now *that* was pretty damn awesome."

She couldn't help but laugh. "Yes, it was."

———◇◇◇◇———

The morning arrived before she knew it, and it was a mad dash to gather her things, to get on the road, and get back to San Francisco in time for her flight.

As she zipped up her suitcase he appeared in the doorway, a small frown creasing his brow. "Don't you need to go?"

She rolled her eyes. "Are you that ready to get rid of me? Geez. I'm almost done." She gave the room one last look. "Okay, let's go."

He picked up the suitcase off the bed and escorted her out of the house. They walked side by side down the path to the garage, and he stowed her luggage in the back of the Jeep. He slammed the trunk closed, and they stood together for maybe a moment longer than strictly necessary. She looked him over, imprinting in her mind the image of him in his jeans and T-shirt and bare feet. "Do you ever wear shoes?"

He shook his head. "Not if I can help it."

"Is that why you left L.A.?" It was something she had wondered about from the very beginning.

He paused, obviously taking his time to think the

question over. "Partially."

She waited for more, but he didn't seem inclined to elaborate and the silence was getting too long. Besides, she needed to be on the road. She opened the driver's door, then looked back at him over her shoulder. "When I make the team, I might need some additional training."

A hint of a smile touched his lips and then was gone. "You have the number."

She squared her shoulders. "I am going to make that team."

He held her gaze. "Yes, you are."

His conviction gave her strength. There were no longer any doubts in her mind. She climbed into the car and winced as her tender bottom settled into the leather seat. "You know, my ass is probably going to sting for weeks."

He closed the door, gave the frame a tap, then stepped back. "Long enough to get you through the trial."

She leaned out the window. There was so much she wanted to say to him, but one word seemed to sum it all up perfectly. "Thanks."

He nodded in reply.

She cranked the ignition and the Jeep roared to life. It was going to be a long drive back to San Francisco. She had a lot to think about. Good stuff. Like how it was going to feel to earn the gold. She gave him a backward wave and followed the curved driveway off his property and onto the road.

DOUBLEHEADER

EMERALD

Doubleheader

Rita looked at the name on the screen and caught her breath. She stared for a few moments before clicking over to an open spreadsheet and entering the name into it. Of course, it had been a possibility ever since he was traded a few months ago to their affiliated major league team. And she had heard about his injury—in the back of her mind, she'd known he might come to the Triple-A level for rehab. But seeing the evidence right in front of her was different from speculation.

Pushing back from her desk, Rita stood and turned to leave the office. For her, one of the biggest perks of working for a professional baseball team was being steps away from a stunning view of the immaculate field whenever she needed to clear her head. As she climbed the steps to the club level on the third base side, she heard the sounds of batting practice underway in preparation for the night's game. She reached the top step and gazed over the field at the array of Triple-A players milling around the batting cage. While she loved the aesthetics of an empty baseball field, the team certainly added to the scenery in a way she appreciated as well.

A few of the players noticed her standing up there and waved. She returned the greeting, giving the manager a nod as he turned and caught sight of her. Despite her desire for a bit of solitary time to process what she'd just seen, Rita turned and headed for the ground level of the field.

"Hi Mike," she greeted the manager as she walked across the track to his position behind the batting cage.

"How goes, Rita?" Mike Ashton, a former all-star left fielder, moved aside to make space for her and turned back to the cage. The familiar sound of bat against ball punctuated the air as they watched the third baseman taking soft warm-up pitches. "Come out to pitch a little batting practice?" he asked with a wink.

Rita laughed. "Not in these heels, thanks." Though her college pitching days were over, she'd been known to engage in exactly what Mike had proposed on more than one occasion. Pitching batting practice wasn't like pitching for real, of course, which was something she did miss. Though her position as vice president and chief financial officer for the team obviously kept her at her desk much of the time, it was no secret she missed playing, and she almost always kept a change of clothes in her office so she could throw a session whenever she had the opportunity.

A not unfamiliar combination of wistfulness and bitterness floated through her as she watched the players who received even the chance to be on this field by virtue of their gender. Almost certainly they took that for granted. She may not have been good enough to make it to the professional level herself—though that was questionable according to some coaches who'd watched her—but she certainly knew women who could have. She would never consider baseball fully integrated until those players got to play alongside the ones she watched now.

The third baseman ended his practice session, and Evan, the starting catcher, stepped into the cage. He looked back at Rita and gave her a wave before turning to the pitcher. Rita returned his enthusiastic smile, responding as usual to the characteristic sweetness in it. Evan was one of her favorite players on the team. Though he'd not yet played at the major league level, it was almost a sure thing he eventually would. She'd miss him when he was gone. As a former pitcher, Rita tended to take note of catchers, and Evan had been no exception when he'd come up from the Double-A team two seasons before. She'd watched Evan closely and even helped him on occasion with drills. She knew how good he was.

"I imagine you saw Chad Tomlinsen will be here tomorrow to rehab his shoulder?"

Rita almost winced at Mike's unexpected comment, but she managed to remain composed.

"I did," she said after a tiny pause.

"I coached him for a while when I was a Double-A batting coach. Be great to see him again and help him get his swing back now that he's healed. He's come a long way since those days."

"As have you." Rita was impressed by how calm her voice sounded. She'd known Mike had been a Double-A batting coach but had had no idea it was with the same team Chad had played for. Baseball was such a small world sometimes.

Mike glanced at her. "You've been around baseball a long time, haven't you? You ever met Tomlinsen?"

Rita swallowed what felt like the orange-sized lump in her throat. "Uh, actually, I have. Way back when. He played at the Single-A level on the team my parents bought the summer after I graduated from college. Haven't seen him in over a decade, though."

Mike grunted before calling out an instruction to Evan at the plate. Evan nodded and adjusted his stance slightly. He sent the next pitch sailing toward center field with a crack, and Mike gave a satisfied nod. Rita swept her gaze over the tangle of players gathered behind the first baseline, hoping the distraction had made Mike forget their conversational thread.

It seemed it had. Evan finished his batting session and walked around the batting cage as Mike broke away to talk to the third base coach.

"Hey, Rita," Evan said with his big smile. Rita returned it and couldn't resist a lightning glance up and down his solid form. Fresh-faced and, in Rita's unbiased perception, ridiculously good-looking, Evan ran a hand over his dark hair as he pulled off his helmet. She realized suddenly that at 23, he was only slightly older than Chad had been when she'd known him. She bit her lip.

"I see you're not dressed to take the field," Evan said with a crooked smile as he moved closer to her. His impish flirtatiousness almost always brought the same out of her, though she was careful to stay on top of it. She would have jumped Evan in a heartbeat under other circumstances, but she did make some effort to maintain a professional decorum and not fuck every player who caught her fancy. It was not a light challenge—despite being around it so much, baseball had never stopped turning her on.

"Not today. I'll let Tim handle batting practice this time around." She nodded at the batting coach, who stood behind the net at the pitcher's mound tossing the ball to whichever player stood at the plate. She chuckled. "You know I prefer pitching for real anyway."

"As usual, I'm happy to catch you any time."

Rita smiled. Evan had indeed shown an endearing willingness to indulge her desire to pitch. While she had played softball in college—the only option open to her as a woman—she had grown up watching baseball, and her father had taught her how to pitch overhand at a young age. She had loved pitching in college and had graduated as the team's ace, but overhand throwing and the smaller size of the baseball were her preference. She made a point of keeping herself in shape and loved any chance to get out on the mound.

"Did you hear Tomlinsen is coming down tomorrow?" Evan was clearly excited by the prospect. Though Chad was no superstar, he had played at the major league level for a few years now and had made a name for himself as a power hitter. Rita resisted the urge to roll her eyes and realized she might be hearing more about Chad in the next 24 hours than she'd realized.

It did make sense to her that Evan would look up to Chad. They played different positions—Chad was a first baseman—but they were both power hitters with similar batting styles. Perhaps most significantly, Chad also played in the major leagues, a privilege Evan had not yet tasted.

"I did hear that, yes. I have to get back to my spreadsheets. Have an awesome game, Evan." Rita smiled.

"Thanks." Evan winked, and she caught him giving her a once-over as she turned to walk off the field. She ignored the heat that ran through her body as a result and headed through the exit, back toward her office.

As she reached it, however, the heat had reached a level of arousal that she knew would not be easy to shake. With a sigh, she sat down, then immediately stood back up and closed her office door. She was going to need some privacy.

Chad Tomlinsen. She looked at the name again on the screen and thought back to the first time she'd ever seen it.

It was the summer after she'd graduated from college and had just returned home. As a woman, Rita's pitching days were over once college was, and it had been time to enter the real world with her brand new business administration degree.

But not before she spent her fair share of time ogling her parents' latest enterprise.

"Dad, who's that?" Rita asked, tapping at her father's shoulder as he spoke to someone standing in the aisle in a suit and tie.

Her father barely glanced down at the player she indicated as he answered, "I don't know, honey. Here, check the program. He'll be listed with his number."

Rita took the slightly crinkled paper her dad passed her and scanned it. Number 28 – Chad Tomlinsen.

She looked back at the unfamiliar player who'd caught her attention. His strong form moved confidently as he sauntered into the on-deck circle, taking a noncommittal swing as he watched the batter dig in.

He hadn't looked at her yet. She found herself determined to make that change.

Rita's email indicator pinged, and she shook herself and checked the computer. It had nothing to do with Chad's imminent arrival this time, and she checked the figure requested, emailed off a confirmation, and sat back to return to her musings.

The way she'd ended up making Chad notice her hadn't exactly been intentional. Bold, yes—once Chad had joined the team that year, she'd walked around a combination of brazen and smitten—but she hadn't really expected that he would notice her. Or at least she'd told herself she hadn't.

The next day, Rita snuck around to the bleachers on the other side of the visitors' dugout and slipped beneath them, taking a moment to let her eyes adjust to the shadows. It was cooler under the bleachers, almost dark despite the sun that blazed unencumbered across the field. The section she had chosen was virtually empty, and no one was around as she leaned back against the narrow metal beam that reached the highest bench above her and faced the field, where the team was taking batting practice. The doors to the stadium hadn't yet been opened to the public.

Chad stood in the vicinity of his position at first base, his eyes apparently on the player taking batting practice. He was alone, most of his teammates gathered nearby or behind the batting cage. Casually he fielded balls when they came to him, tossing them over to the third baseman, who appeared to also be practicing fielding, before turning back toward the plate. His sunglasses made it impossible to tell exactly where he was looking but, here in the shadows all the way on the other side of the field, Rita was confident she wasn't visible to him.

She had a baseball in her hand. Bringing it to her face, she inhaled the scent of fresh leather and arched her back, sliding her other hand down the side of her tank top. Her eyes flicked around her again. She was alone in the section; the nearest people to her seemed to be those on the field, and they were a considerable distance away.

Rita slid the ball down the front of her, between her breasts over her top and down to the crotch of her cutoffs. She stole another glance around and paused as the crack of a bat was followed by one of the small white balls scampering Chad's way. He fielded it easily *and threw it across the field to his teammate.*

Suddenly he turned his head just slightly, and Rita froze, consumed by the inexplicable feeling he had spotted her. She swallowed and stayed still, the ball clutched in her right hand resting now against her belly. Chad's sunglasses belied the target of his actual gaze, and a second later he moved seamlessly to field another ball. If he had seen her, he'd shown no indication. Rita decided it was a false alarm and that she was just a bit jumpy under the circumstances.

Of course, as she returned to her deviance after another furtive look around, she realized it wasn't as though she'd actually be opposed to Chad watching her. She roved her eyes across the field, checking with a fluttering in her stomach to see if any of his teammates had seemed to catch sight of her in the shadow of the opposite-field bleachers. But they, like Chad, were focused on the batter as Rita slipped a finger beneath the button of her cutoffs.

Her intake of breath was sharp as she popped the button and pulled down the zipper. At that moment she felt most aware of the risk of her position, and she stopped to take another good look around before she began to focus more strongly on other things.

She let her cutoffs drop and slipped her fingers into her panties. Eventually she slipped them to the side and held them with the fingers of her left hand, her pussy exposed to the darkened air under the bleachers.

With the removal of all such obstacles, Rita slid the baseball down over the front of her body so it eventually covered her clit. Maneuvering her wrist deftly, she found a rhythm that made her bite her lip and arch her back as she rolled the ball against the increasingly sensitive spot.

With yet another glance around, Rita switched the ball to her other hand and plunged her fingers inside herself to finish the job. She shook as she came, dropping the ball to grab the beam behind her for support as her legs threatened to give out.

Panting, she shifted her panties back into place and rebuttoned her cutoffs. As she looked up, Chad subtly adjusted his crotch, and Rita froze again. But the gesture was a common one in baseball, and with another check on his teammates, she again felt assured of her secrecy. Still working to catch her breath, she picked up the ball and blinked as she crept back out into the sunlight. With a final sweep of her gaze over the immediate surroundings, she squared her shoulders and walked back toward the concourse as though nothing was amiss.

As she reached the concrete steps up to the stadium exit, she turned back a final time to look at Chad. She caught her breath a little as she saw that his head was turned, directed straight at her as his mouth twisted in the tiniest of sly smiles. The minuscule incline of his head made it unmistakable this time that he was looking at her.

Rita's heart jumpstarted like the line drive that had just been smacked into the outfield, and she nearly dropped the ball in her hand. Had he seen? Would he say something? What was going to happen?

Before she could even acknowledge his gaze, Chad turned back to his teammate at the plate as the next pitch was delivered. Rita whirled and almost ran from the stadium.

Rita shook her head now as she thought about what might have happened had she been caught. At the time, she'd had a cocky—and no doubt misguided—idea that she would have been able to waylay any repercussions due to her parents' ownership of the team. She could hardly remember what the hell she'd been thinking then and felt immensely grateful she'd never had to test that theory, the inaccuracy of which she could only imagine.

Nonetheless, she'd stayed away from the stadium for nearly a week, fearful that Chad may not have been the only one who'd seen her or that he would choose to spill the beans to anyone who happened by. When there was nary a peep out of her parents or anyone else about the owners' daughter having been seen masturbating under the bleachers, she made her next appearance at a home game, her brazenness now slightly in check—but no less smitten.

Rita sighed and leaned back in her chair. Despite her unabashed interest in Chad, there had been an obstacle in the way of pursuing him just as unabashedly. Its name was Blake.

Closing her eyes, Rita rubbed her forehead. The introduction of her ex-husband's name into her reminiscences didn't feel particularly welcome. Standing, she reached to shut down her computer, then grabbed her purse and extracted her keys, flicking off the light as she pulled open the office door.

"Mike said you knew Tomlinsen back when he was in Single-A," Tom Rollins, the principal team owner, said from his seat in the owner's box as they watched the top of the first inning. At the last minute, Rita had tabled her plan to skip the game and head home, so she now stood beside Tom, close to the glass, watching as Evan called time out and ran to the mound to clarify something with the pitcher. She could hardly believe Chad's name had come up again; one would think they never saw major league players come down to Triple-A or something.

"Yes," she said, taking a swig from the beer bottle in her hand and hoping for a change of subject. Despite herself, she smiled as she recalled hearing the news of her parents' impending team ownership. They'd been on the phone during the spring of her final semester. She was thrilled to hear of the development, of course, and said something to her mother about all the hot baseball players she'd get to meet.

She could almost see the disapproving look her mother must have been sporting when she said huffily, "I assure you that did *not* factor into our decision. We're not *buying* you a husband, Rita."

Her mother hadn't been privy Rita's smirk: as though "husband" had anything to do with it.

Rita took another sip of her beer and stared out at the field. As it turned out, the "husband" bit had more to do with it than she'd realized. Just not in the way her mother meant.

Tom continued the conversation with the general manager who stood nearby and Rita tuned out, hoping her part in it was over. Her eyes narrowed as her thoughts returned to the past. The on-again, off-again relationship she'd had with Blake throughout high school had entered an "on" phase upon her return home after graduation—and just before she met Chad. The month immediately following her little soirée under the bleachers had been fraught with the frustration of seeing Chad regularly but not getting to pursue him due to her relationship with Blake.

Until they'd fallen back into yet another "off" period, and everything had changed.

Rita excused herself and exited the owner's box. Finishing her beer, she dropped the bottle in a recycling bin and wandered over to the stairs to the upper deck. Ascending them, she emerged into the view of the emerald field from above and leaned against the wall across from where an usher was usually stationed. Upon the usher's return, she would be requested to show her ticket or asked to move, she was sure, but for the time being, she stood and viewed the field from afar.

The day she'd actually met Chad was more than a month after she'd made herself come watching him under the bleachers—and only a few days after she and Blake had said yet again that they were through.

Rita turned at the sound of her name. The starting catcher, whom she'd quickly befriended amidst detailed talk of pitches and delivery, was waving at her as he made his way to where she stood beside the fence near the dugout.

"Hi Randy," she greeted him, then stopped short as Chad came out of the dugout and stood at his side.

"Have you met Chad?" Randy said easily, gesturing to the blond man beside him. Rita's eyes felt frozen on him as she stared up at him, and she desperately hoped this wasn't as obvious as it seemed to her. Chad met her gaze, a combination of intensity, curiosity, and, most of all, recognition in the blue eyes that held hers.

"Glad to finally meet you, Rita," he said as he shook her hand. She sensed his breathing change slightly as he said, "Pretty sure I've seen you around."

Taking a deep breath, Rita concentrated on transforming her nervous energy and embarrassment into seductiveness. After all, hadn't she thought at the time that she wouldn't really have minded if he saw her? And now it wasn't as though there was anything stopping her from going after what she'd wanted all along.

"Yes, I make my appearances here and there," she said. "My parents own the team."

Surprise flashed in Chad's eyes, followed by understanding. "I see. Guess that means you pretty much have the run of the place, then, huh?"

"Something like that." Rita met his eyes and grew wet at the overt desire she saw in them.

They'd fucked that night in the parking lot after the game, then much later in the clubhouse, owner's box, and behind the dugout. Mostly, though, Chad hadn't wanted to engage in such risky public behavior, which Rita could understand. He had far more to lose than she did if they were caught.

In fact, Chad hadn't really wanted anyone to know about their relationship, feeling it could look like a conflict of interest for him to be fucking the team owners' daughter. "You know they don't have any influence over your actual career, right?" she'd asked him once. "The major league office is the only place those decisions get made, and they couldn't care less what my parents say."

"I know," he'd answered. "I just … I just I feel like it doesn't look right."

Rita had had her own reasons for not wanting to flaunt their relationship. Upon casually mentioning her interest in Chad while having dinner with her parents one night, her father had sounded a cautionary note.

"Players aren't really people you want to get involved with like that, Rita. They're focused on their career, and most of them won't make it big, though they'll be bent on trying for years to come. It's not a very stable environment." He smiled. "Besides, you and Blake aren't really over, are you?" His knowing look shifted to include her mother as he spoke, apparently ignoring the grimace on Rita's face. "I don't know what we'd do if Blake wasn't eventually an official part of our family."

Her mother's gentle laugh of agreement floated across the table as she too smiled warmly at her daughter.

Her parents sure had seemed concerned with marriage and stability—two things Rita hadn't really been focused on at all.

Still, for their own respective reasons, she and Chad had kept quiet about their blossoming relationship. Aside from sneaking in a few quickies in the clubhouse now and then, or on the bus after the team returned from being on the road, most of their carnal encounters had taken place away from the stadium—albeit not entirely away from public spaces.

Rita started now as a roar shook the crowd inside the stadium. She made her way back in and saw a player jogging the bases, indicating a home run had just been hit. Squinting, she made out the number 17 on the back of the jersey and smiled. It was Evan, and she joined in the cheering around her as he made his way home, grinning, and walked into a round of high fives in the dugout.

It had been about a month later that things had started to shift again.

Chad was flushed—he looked as animated as he had after she'd sucked his cock on the clubhouse couch, both of them listening for any sounds of someone coming as she'd knelt in front him and he'd shoved her head down rhythmically the way he knew she loved.

"What?" she said, his obvious excitement bringing a grin to her lips.

"I'm moving up—and I got traded." Chad was so excited he was out of breath. "I'll have to move to Minnesota, and next

week I'll be playing Double-A."

Rita's jaw dropped. She leapt into his arms, thrilled for him even as her stomach twisted at the distance Minnesota represented.

"I want you to come with me," Chad said before she'd even disentangled herself. Rita froze. He pulled back and held her so he could look at her. "I want you to move with me."

Rita's heart pounded as she remembered her father's words back when she'd first mentioned Chad to them. She hadn't told Chad that Blake had been pursuing her again. She couldn't deny the connection she felt with Blake—there was a reason they'd been together on and off since high school—but she'd been keeping her distance because of what she had going on with Chad. The discomfort of uncertainty rushed her system, and she moved forward to hug Chad again so he wouldn't see it on her face.

Blake had indeed become an official part of the family, and Chad had moved on to Double-A baseball in Minnesota. She hadn't dwelled very much on how things might have been different or why she'd made the choices she had when Blake proposed at the end of that summer. Chad, for his part, had done well professionally in the last decade. He'd moved up quickly to Triple-A from Double-A. After a few years there, he'd been called up to the majors. His first two years had been sporadic, with the not uncommon circumstance of being called up and sent down throughout both seasons. For a few years following that, he'd been a solid backup player in the major leagues, filling in at first base when needed and sometimes serving as the designated hitter.

Eventually, he made his way to starter status.

And he would be in this very stadium the next day. Rita pushed away from the wall and walked slowly as she made her way to the parking lot, unsure whether she dreaded or yearned to show up at work the next day.

◇◇◇◇

Rita stayed in her office as much as she could the following day, until hunger trumped her nervous reticence sometime in the early afternoon. She left her office and took the elevator down to the main concourse, surreptitiously looking around as she scurried through the open space.

As she headed around the main concourse and neared the stairs that led down to the clubhouse level, she saw him approaching from the other direction. His head was down, and the brim of his hat mostly blocked his face from her view. His glove dangled from the fingers of his right hand, and his cleats ground against the concrete with each step.

In the split-second it took her to recognize him, her breath escaped her. She stood there trying to catch it, realizing at the last second that she'd better move if she didn't want to encounter him, as she was standing directly in his line of vision were he to raise his head.

Too late. Just as her muscles started working again, Chad did exactly that. His eyes landed on hers with a neutral friendliness for a fraction of a second before recognition washed over them.

He stopped short. Rita was nowhere close to having found her voice yet.

Chad's eyes stayed on her for several seconds, and she could almost see his internal process of shock, bafflement, and, eventually, comprehension of what she might be doing there.

"Rita," he said finally, stepping forward but not extending his hand or doing anything else to initiate physical contact between them.

She managed a nod, drawing a deep breath before responding in kind. "Hi, Chad."

"You work here?" His voice didn't sound nearly as strangled as she felt hers did, but when she spoke, she realized she sounded far more composed than she felt.

"Yes."

Chad gave a nod but didn't speak.

Rita straightened slightly. "I'm the CFO."

Chad held her gaze. "You knew I would be coming then, I take it."

She swallowed. He was right, of course. She realized it hadn't even occurred to her that he would know that when he found out her position with the team.

"I did. How's your shoulder?"

She saw a tiny flash in Chad's eyes, and her mouth twisted into a slight involuntary grimace of empathy. Injuries that kept them from the game were one of the hardest things players endured. Having undergone her share of them during her college days, she had some idea of how it felt.

"It's feeling okay. Doctor says I'm ready for full batting practice and a game or two as the designated hitter." Chad nodded, then said gruffly, "Thanks for asking."

He'd repeated what his major league manager had told the press, and Rita knew it. She wanted to say that she knew that what the doctor said didn't matter as much as how he felt, which was what she'd been seeking when she asked, but suddenly the clarification felt too intimate somehow, too personal. She let the inquiry drop and gathered her wits. As she did, she saw Chad's eyes flick up and down her body, fast enough that she might have missed it if she'd been blinking. She was startled by the way her breath left her again, almost as intensely as it had when she'd first seen him moments before. But she could tell the action on his part was not meant to be noticed—for all she knew, it could have been automatic or even accidental. She cleared her throat.

"Well, nice to see you, Chad. I have to run."

He nodded, already stepping toward the stairs that went down to the clubhouse. "Yeah," he said, pointing his glove at her before swinging it around to his other hand and beginning his descent. "See you around, Rita." The crunch of his cleats echoed then receded down the cavernous hallway.

◇◇◇

Rita had underestimated how difficult she would find it to concentrate on work once she knew Chad was in the building. Of course, she hadn't known what it would be like to see him until she did. She swallowed, reaching for a spreadsheet on her desk in a hopeless effort to distract herself. She put it down almost as soon as she picked it up and told herself she needed to face the facts: she wanted to fuck Chad as much as she ever had.

That, she realized, had never changed. But it was arguably even less appropriate now, for both of them, than it had been a decade ago. Just as she'd had to do with a number of other players, she was just going to have to get used to spending several hours a day in the same building with people whom she wanted to jump like a jackrabbit in heat.

Of course, those other players didn't know how to fuck her exactly the way she liked: a little bit rough with one fist gripping hair, their other hand holding both of hers above her head. She liked a good strong grip …

Rita shoved her chair back and left her office. She would go for a walk, like she usually did when she felt distracted. Looking at a baseball field was unlikely to do anything to lower the arousal in her, but sitting at her desk letting her mind run away with itself obviously wasn't working either.

She rode the elevator down to the main floor. As she stepped out, the music from the sound system on the field began to blare, signifying that batting practice was about to start.

As she reached the corner of the hallway that led to the clubhouse tunnel, the music abruptly stopped and she overheard a familiar voice.

"No, she's not married. Divorced, I think."

Rita stopped in her tracks. She recognized the voice as Evan's, but she couldn't tell if they were coming her way or standing still somewhere around the corner. Before she could decide what to do, someone responded.

"I see. How long have you known her?"

It was Chad.

"Since I got here a couple years ago. She's been working here a while, I think." Evan gave a little laugh. "I've wanted her since the second I saw her, of course. But I leave it alone. Always felt like I should stay away from somebody in that kind of position. I sure would like to have her, though. But it seems like things could get fucked up quickly if it went wrong."

Rita found herself barely breathing. She looked around for somewhere to duck out of sight, but the hallway stretched behind her, and moving forward would place her face-to-face with this conversation.

"You know," Evan continued, as though Chad was somehow not understanding. "A conflict of interest. Like—"

"I understand conflict of interest," Chad said gruffly. It was clear from his tone that the conversation was over, though Evan wouldn't have known just how well Chad understood.

Music blasted out again, and Rita used its cover to mask her footsteps as she whirled around and strode back up the hallway, not taking a full breath until she had turned another corner and reached the flight of steps that led back up to her office.

⬦⬦⬦⬦

Rita brought lunch with her the next day and didn't leave the floor her office was on until it was time to go home for the day. She knew batting practice was well underway as she took the elevator down a floor and walked quickly across the concourse, keys in hand.

"Rita," a voice called, and she turned to see Tom walking toward her. "Did you get those figures reconciled for the compensations of the two Double-A players called up last week?"

"Yes." Rita was relieved that she had indeed found the source of the discrepancy and gotten it fixed. She didn't really need anyone noticing how distracted she'd seemed lately or concluding that it seemed to coincide with Chad's arrival.

Tom, unfortunately, seemed keen to continue chatting and turned automatically toward the entrance to the field as Rita held back a sigh and fell into step beside him. The doors hadn't yet been opened to the public for the night's game, and the stands were mostly empty as she and Tom walked onto the field and stopped on the fringes of the batting taking place at home plate.

Rita tried to keep her eyes averted and focus on what Tom was saying, but her gaze involuntarily strayed to the cluster of white uniforms behind the batting cage. Her breath caught as she saw the number 28 on the back of one of them. He was facing away from her and likely hadn't seen her yet.

At that moment Evan, who was crossing the field from the bullpen, called a greeting to her. Chad turned around and looked at her. She looked back, her eyes moving back and forth between Chad and Evan as the latter neared and said hello to Tom. Tom greeted him heartily before turning to talk to Mike, and Rita resisted the urge to scream as she found herself in the exact situation she had been determined to avoid all day. She hadn't even wanted to find herself on the field at all.

Chad was still looking at her, and Evan had stopped approximately between them. She nodded and stepped forward, unsure how to exit gracefully. Though neither of them, after all, knew she'd overheard them the previous day.

"Hello, Chad. Evan." She nodded at both of them. Despite the awkwardness she felt, she couldn't deny the rush of heat that coursed through her, and she willed her rising blush to disappear.

"Oh, have you two met already?" Evan said in his friendly way, looking from Rita to Chad.

"We have," Chad answered before Rita could speak. "Long ago, as a matter of fact."

"Really?" Evan looked confused, which Rita could understand given his conversation with Chad the day before. She surmised that he hadn't actually said anything about knowing her.

"Yes," Chad said, finally tearing his eyes from Rita

to look at Evan. "Rita's parents owned the Single-A team I played for when I was first signed."

"No kidding." Evan suddenly seemed to pick up on something in Chad's gaze, and for the first time, he appeared uncomfortable. "Well, I'm up soon," he said, gesturing at the batting cage behind him. "Talk to you later, Rita." He nodded at Chad and went to join some of his teammates along the batting cage.

Rita looked at Chad. "Were you sending him some kind of 'back off' signals only perceptible by testosterone or something?" she asked dryly.

Chad's eyes were hard as he held her gaze. Rita clenched her teeth as she felt her stomach tighten—it was the same look he used to give her before he took her the rough way she loved. Though she hadn't seen it in more than ten years, she remembered that look like it was yesterday. With all her effort, she maintained a social decorum rather than commanding Chad to fuck her right there. The annoyance she felt with him didn't seem to hinder one bit how simultaneously turned on she felt.

"Should I have been?" Chad finally answered. He wasn't smiling, and Rita didn't know how to read the look in his eyes.

She also didn't know how to answer. After a long pause, she decided to deflect and said, "He looks up to you, you know. You have the kind of home run record he aspires to at the major league level someday."

After a beat, during which she sensed Chad wrestled

with the option of pursuing unanswered questions, her former lover nodded and said, "He's a good kid. Smart, too. He'll make it to the big leagues eventually."

"Yes, he will," Rita agreed. "Perhaps someday you'll play together."

"We're already playing together right here." Chad's gaze was steady, and for some reason the words called up another blush in Rita. "So, to get off the subject of Evan for a moment, I hear you're not married anymore?"

Rita caught her breath. "That's correct," she said, suddenly wanting to be anywhere but right there. But when she met Chad's eyes again, the wish turned instantaneously to a pure desire for Chad's cock inside her. It was so strong she had to turn away.

After the moment passed—barely—and she reined in her unwitting impulses, she turned back to him. "What about you? Are you married?" She realized the question hadn't even occurred to her before now, and she found herself holding her breath as she waited for his answer.

"No."

Mike chose that moment to call Chad over for batting practice, and Chad waved at him and stepped forward. "Gotta run," he said over his shoulder, his eyes flicking up and down her body before meeting her gaze again. "Catch you later."

"Have a great game," she called after him. She watched as he moved to the batter's box and prepared to take the first pitch. She was struck by how familiar his stance was and, for about the hundredth time in the past 72 hours, she found herself transported again back to that Single-A stadium in her hometown, watching with a tingling in her pussy as Chad went to bat, anticipating the pounding to which she would be treated just hours later. Chad's swing made contact, and the cracking sound jolted her back to the present—where she found herself just as wet as she had been back then.

She turned to walk off the field but stopped when she heard Evan call to her.

"Hey," he said, panting slightly as he ran up. With a glance back at Chad in the batting cage, he said, "Um—." Then he stopped, clearly uncomfortable.

"What's up?" Rita prompted.

Evan paused before saying, "Well, I just wanted to tell you I didn't know you and Chad knew each other. I— well, I kind of—" Evan fiddled with the hat in his hands, looking shyer than she'd ever seen him. She waited for him to go on as Chad hit a home run over the left field wall. "Earlier today, I kind of confided to him that I have a … a little bit of a crush on you," he finished in a rush, and Rita bit back a smile. "A little bit of a crush." That was one way to put what she'd overheard him convey.

"And I just hope …" Evan went on, his discomfort still evident. "I mean, I don't know how you two know each other or how well or whatever." Evan was blushing so much Rita found herself searching for something that would help put him at ease. He continued before she could say anything.

"I just hope I didn't piss him off or anything. I'd hate to antagonize someone I—well, someone like that. I mean, it would be a dream come true to play on a team with Chad in the big leagues." Evan's combination of awe and distress made Rita want to hug him.

"I don't think you should worry about it, Evan. I'm sure Chad thinks highly of you—he's seen you play, and it's obvious how good you are—and he wouldn't let anything about what you said impact that."

"Well …" Evan broke off, and she realized suddenly there was more on his mind than perhaps Chad had perceived. He really did want to know what the history was between them—and perhaps if any of that history still lingered.

Rita blushed slightly. She was certainly finding herself at a loss for what to say a lot lately. This time, she was saved by a signal from Mike that it was time for the team to head into the clubhouse. With a rushed nod at her, Evan turned and jogged toward the dugout, blending in with the rest of the white uniforms that now clustered around the steps. Chad was one of the last ones, and he threw a glance Rita's way as he descended into the dugout. Just before he looked away, his lips turned up into a small smile uncannily like the one she'd first seen on him—except that this time it seemed grudging instead of sly.

Rita put her keys back into her purse and headed to the box to watch the game.

◇◇◇◇

As the next day was a rare day off for the team, Rita took advantage of the chance to wander out after work and look at the field void of any occupants. The stadium's emptiness was almost eerie juxtaposed with the crowd that had turned out for the previous night's victory. Rita smiled as she remembered Chad's double in the fifth-inning—his swing looked great, and she could tell he felt no pain in his shoulder. He would return to the majors in a day or two. Rita liked to think things would return to normal then, but she somehow doubted that would be the case. Chad knew where she was now, and they'd broken their ten-year silence—and beyond that, there was Evan's attraction to her to contend with.

All of it was going to make any ideas about not getting involved (as rarely as possible, anyway) with her own players a hell of a lot more challenging.

She moved along the seats and down the steps back into the main concourse. Catching sight of a poster depicting one of their starting pitchers, she stopped in front of it. Automatically, her fingers moved as though they were tightening over a ball. Some twelve years later she still yearned to hold the ball in her hand, feel the seams under her fingertips as she readied to deliver her hardest shot past the batter that stood between her and her target. There was little that matched the adrenaline rush she got from winding up and letting fly all the energy in her body through a little white leather ball. It became like a comet that took everything she had inside her and hurled it away into a safe leather space designed specifically for it. Whatever it was she was feeling, she could channel it into that ball and watch it transform, dissolve, explode, or whatever she wanted it to do. It had rarely failed her.

Though she had loved softball and played it well, baseball had always been where her heart was.

"Take you back, does it?"

Rita jumped. When she turned, she saw Chad striding toward her dressed in warm-up gear. She realized she shouldn't be surprised to see him here. Even though there wasn't a game, it would still make sense for him to do some off-day rehab for his shoulder.

"I'm here working with Tim and icing the shoulder," Chad supplied, as though reading her mind. "Your buddy Evan is here too, doing drills with the bench coach in the bullpen," he added with a tiny smirk.

Rita returned it. "That's nice to know. You haven't been giving him a hard time, have you?"

"Of course not." The sarcasm dropped from Chad's voice as he looked at her like she should know better. Rita looked away. The look reminded her of the fundamental kindness she had always seen in Chad, regardless of whatever hardness he might convey on the surface. While kindness wasn't always an inherent aphrodisiac for her, at that moment, on some level, she realized it was.

Granted, at this point she might as well acknowledge that Chad himself seemed to be a walking aphrodisiac.

He was still looking at her. "Walk me to the clubhouse?"

he asked casually. She agreed, suddenly wondering what he had been doing in this area of the stadium following his workout. She decided to let the question pass.

"So. You like working for the team?" he asked as they crossed the empty expanse of concrete.

"Yeah," she said. Chad didn't respond. He seemed to be waiting for her to say more.

"I mean, I love the game ... as you know," she continued. She thought about the poster she'd just seen, and her fingers felt empty again for a moment. "Of course, I'd rather be playing," she blurted.

"Yeah," Chad said, as though this didn't surprise him at all. "I remember your talking about that back when ... back when we knew each other."

"You do?" For some reason this surprised her. She did remember expressing her frustration that, for her, playing baseball was over; while for him, the chance to make a living at it was just beginning. Whether or not she was good enough wasn't the point. She didn't even get the chance to find out. It hadn't occurred to her that Chad would remember that.

"Of course. You talked about it all the time."

"Did I?" Rita wondered aloud. They'd reached the ramp that led to the clubhouse tunnel, and Rita heard another set of cleats somewhere within. Momentarily, Evan came into view.

"Hi, guys," he said with an easy smile. His concern about Chad seemed to have dissipated, and Rita was relieved. Not that she had doubted Chad when he'd said he wasn't giving Evan the cold shoulder, but it was nice to see affirming evidence.

"What's up?" he asked as the three of them met and stopped near the clubhouse door. His eyes shifted to Rita. "Done for the day?"

"Yes." Then, spontaneously, she added, "You want to catch me for a bit?" The urge to throw the ball was pulsing in her—along with perhaps something else—and the words bubbled up almost before she was aware of them.

"Sure," Evan said.

Rita turned to Chad. "Want a little extra batting practice?"

"Who am I to turn down the chance to see you pitch?" Chad drawled.

"Great. I have to change. I'll meet you at the clubhouse entrance in a few."

Back in her office, Rita felt the low but unmistakable adrenaline buzz coursing through her as she tied her shoes. She reached to the top of a file cabinet and grabbed her glove. It was the same one she'd used when she'd played, and she'd kept it in every office she'd ever had as she worked her way up the administrative side of professional baseball.

Evan and Chad were waiting for her outside the clubhouse door.

"I think Tim was maybe going to work with Miguel for a while on the field, so we should probably use the batting cage," Evan said as she followed them inside.

They made their way to the indoor batting cage and

filed in. Evan set a bucket of balls near the pitching area while Rita stretched a little. Chad took a few practice swings nearby.

When she was ready, Rita grabbed a ball and threw it into her glove. She tossed a couple of light pitches to Evan, who squatted behind the plate, before she got into position for real. She took a deep breath, let it out hard, and wound up.

The ball smacked into Evan's glove, and Rita felt the unique power of firing an overhand fastball fill her body. Evan threw the ball back to her, and she repositioned and eyeballed the plate. Her next pitch went very close to where she'd wanted it to, and she couldn't hold back a grin.

"Nice slider," Evan called as he tossed the ball back to her.

After a few more pitches, she looked over at Chad. "Ready?"

Chad, she noticed, looked a bit taken aback. She wondered suddenly why he had never seen her pitch that summer years ago. Perhaps because she hadn't had a catcher handy to present the opportunity.

Chad positioned himself at the plate, and Rita wound up and let fly. A crack filled the narrow enclosure as Chad made contact and sent the ball into the net above Rita's head. She picked up another ball from the bucket and repeated the process. Soon she worked into a rhythm, the intricacy of the process taking over—ball, plant, wind-up, release, follow-through—and she and the men at the plate moved as a system, each fulfilling his or her role like a smoothly running machine. Chad hit most of what she threw, but she got a few past him, too. Her body felt like it was waking up, freeing an energy she only ever felt when she was on the mound.

As she threw, that energy mixed with the not-unfamiliar sensation of frustration and longing. The hard fact was, unlike the men to whom she was pitching, she didn't get to suit up every day and come out to do this—not only do it, but make her living doing it. Of course, she made her living through baseball in another way. But she'd give up any of the perks and privileges she'd seen in all her days at the executive level for the chance simply to play on the field.

She jumped out of the way as Chad hit a line drive a few feet to her left. Grabbing the final ball in the bucket, she made eye contact with Evan and paused. He guessed her intention correctly and moved the glove where she would place one of her sliders. She looked away and took a breath, then wound up, looked right where she wanted the ball to go, and fired, flicking her wrist a fraction of an inch at the last second.

Chad took a power swing, and the ball went straight into the glove. He looked back at her and smirked, tapping the end of the bat against his toe. "Yeah, nice one, honey."

Rita was out of breath. Excitement, exertion, and something else coursed through her as she picked up the bucket beside her. "Empty," she said as she carried it forward to pick up the balls that had gotten past Evan or that Chad

had fouled back. Chad tossed the bat aside, and Evan lifted off his mask and stood up. Rita took advantage of their momentary distraction to unabashedly run her eyes over their forms in turn. Her breath deepened.

Evan had just finished taking off the rest of his catching gear when she reached the plate and dropped the bucket. Chad tossed two balls into it and turned to her. Before he could speak, she stepped forward and kissed him hard. Chad fell back a step, his arms catching her around the waist and holding tight as she devoured him. After a second she broke off and turned to Evan, whose jaw hung limply as he watched them from a couple feet away.

She stepped toward him and, without preamble, grabbed his crotch. His eyes widened, and his mouth opened further for a second before he snapped it shut and swallowed.

He was wearing a cup, of course, but Rita squeezed anyway. She looked back at Chad. "Do you have condoms in your locker?"

He seemed at a loss for words for a second, then gave a short twitch of his head. "No."

She turned to Evan. "Do you?"

Evan took a little longer to regain the power of speech. After a few seconds he sputtered, "Um … yes. I do."

Rita dropped her hands from both of them. "Why don't you go get them."

Evan stared at her, and she held his gaze. He moved forward incrementally, and Rita could tell he wanted to kiss her. Instead, he stepped aside and almost jogged to the entrance of the batting cage. "Be right back," he tossed over his shoulder as he disappeared.

She and Chad stood silently, both facing the door through which Evan had disappeared. Rita's breath was shallow, arousal heating her face and dampening her panties, threatening to waylay her senses.

After a moment, Chad spoke.

"Still like things the way you did back then?" He didn't look at her but rather continued to stare straight ahead where Evan had gone, as though watching for him to come back.

There was no need to ask what he meant. She swallowed as she felt herself get wet—or wetter, as the case may be.

"Yeah."

Chad nodded once as the door opened and Evan came rushing back in. He had left his glove behind and held one hand now in a fist at his side. Rita smiled.

"We're going to my office." She turned on her heel and led the way through the tunnel and up the ramp.

They didn't speak as their steps echoed across the concrete floor. The sun had long since set, and the concourse was dark as they made their way around the stadium to the stairs that led up to the offices. Rita could feel the heat from Chad's body beside her, and it almost made her lightheaded. She had a feeling that Evan, on the other side, was still too stunned to speak even if she were to speak directly to him.

She didn't turn on the lights in her office. She just

motioned them in silently and locked the door behind them. Then she took a deep breath and turned around.

She leaned back against the door even before Chad stepped forward and pushed her against it, his lips solid against the side of her neck as he pulled her shirt up, backing away only to pull it over her head. She reached a hand out to Evan, who stepped forward and received it, then tentatively reached up and covered her breast with his other hand, squeezing harder when she moaned a little into the otherwise silent air of the office.

Chad pulled her forward, and Rita dropped eagerly to her knees, sliding her hand down Evan's body as she did. Chad already had his cock out by the time she hit the floor, and she dove forward to take it her mouth, fumbling with her other hand to extract Evan's from his pants. She felt him help, and when it was free, she stroked it slowly while she sucked Chad at the same pace, her fingers lingering against his balls.

Chad ran a hand through her hair. For a brief second she felt his thumb brush across her cheek, and she caught her breath for a reason other than unrelenting lust. There was no mistaking the tenderness in the movement, and it surprised her, but it was gone almost before she'd had time to process it.

She sucked him deeper, looking up at him as he wound his hand into a fist in her hair. His breath deepened as his eyes darkened with helpless arousal, and she knew she could make him come that way in a matter of seconds if she worked at it.

Chad pulled her back by her hair and turned her around. "Suck his dick now, baby," he said, pushing her head toward Evan's cock, which Evan eagerly helped to slip between her lips. "That's right," Chad whispered as he kept his grip and pushed her head rhythmically. "Good girl."

It had been so long since she'd been called a "good girl"—just over ten years, in fact—that Rita almost came at the words. She'd never told anyone else what the phrase did for her, and it clearly hadn't lost its power. Chad reached down and pulled her up by her torso, maintaining his hold on her head so that Evan's penis remained in her mouth. He let go only to pull off her shorts and panties, and to pull up a nearby chair for her to kneel on for support. Rita did so, resting forward against the back of the chair as she took Evan's cock to the back of her throat.

For a moment, Chad removed his hands from her. As she heard him rip open a condom, Rita had to pull away from Evan for a second to catch her breath, aware that she could come any second. She looked up at Evan, whose eyes held the desperate hunger of youth and sweetness. She gave him a sly smile, and he pulled her up and kissed her, his eager tongue exploring urgently as his hand slipped around the back of her neck.

She felt Chad's hands on her hips, and in a second he had slipped into her. She moaned into Evan's mouth, arching her back to take Chad as deep as she could in her position. Chad gave her a second to get used to him, running his hands slowly up and down her back, around her torso and caressing her breasts. Her shudder at his touch gave away just how much she had missed it.

Then, without warning, he began pistoning forcefully into her. Rita pulled away from Evan and cried out, moving beyond any form of rational thought as Chad reached around and found her clit. She didn't even register when she started coming, she just knew she was, and she screamed incoherently as her body bucked around Chad's cock, catching herself on the back of the chair as she fell forward.

She heard Chad's voice but didn't register what he said, and seconds later Evan's hands found her head and guided her mouth gently back to his cock. She was happy to take it, sucking blissfully amidst the endorphins that floated like snow-globe glitter in her brain as Chad fucked her none too gently from behind. He gave her ass a heavy slap, and she grunted against Evan's cock.

"She loves it," she heard Chad say this time, and she smiled as best she could with Evan filling her mouth as she pictured the questioning look of concern from Evan that had probably prompted the comment.

"I'm gonna come, baby," Chad murmured, reaching out to grab her hair again and almost pulling her off Evan in his fervor. "Are you ready for that? You ready for me to shoot this load deep inside you?"

Rita squealed against Evan's cock and she heard his intake of breath at the increased stimulation. Chad grabbed both her hips and slammed into her, hissing a long

"Fuuuuck" as she felt him release and push inside her as deeply as he could go. Chad bucked and pumped behind her, as she released Evan's cock from her mouth. She took it in one hand and stroked it smoothly as her breath stuttered, her clit aching to be touched again as Chad eventually pulled out of her.

"All right, come on baby," Chad panted softly as he pulled her up and moved the chair. "Lie down and let Evan fuck you."

Rita slid like water to the ground and lay on her back, her clit pulsing insistently as she anticipated Evan's cock. Evan, for his part, didn't need to be told twice as he dropped to his knees and fumbled with the condom Chad handed to him.

"Spread your legs for him, baby," Chad whispered unnecessarily as Evan moved into position and slid inside her.

"Oh, god," she gasped as the younger man's cock filled her. Evan covered her body with his as he dropped forward onto his elbows, sliding both hands into her hair with a gentleness that contradicted the urgency of his cock as it pounded into her. His breath was harsh in her ear as she wrapped her legs around his waist and pulled him in deeper.

"Rita," he whispered almost inaudibly as the speed of his thrusting increased. A second later he gripped her hair tightly as he came, slamming into her with abandon as she squeezed his hard shoulders and held back another cry.

"Finish her off, Evan," Chad murmured as Evan

pushed himself up. With a little smile Rita could only attribute to amusement at Chad's telling him what to do, Evan slid his fingers down to her slick clit and brushed it gently, oh so gently, making every nerve in her body stand on end.

A tiny "Oh" emerged from Rita's mouth as her breath paused. One more movement from Evan's finger and she was going to come. The moment seemed to suspend itself in her darkened office as her body coiled, nearly shaking in anticipation of the release it so needed.

Evan's finger moved a fraction of an inch, and Rita screamed as the orgasm flooded through her, feeling the pace of Evan's finger increasing as she thrashed beneath him. For what seemed like minutes she writhed and shrieked, finally covering Evan's hand with her own to still it when she couldn't take anymore. She gulped air, her body shuddering as she worked to catch her breath. An involuntary giggle emerged from the pure ecstasy deluging her system, and Chad, who had at some point moved to the floor to kneel beside her, caught her hand as it fell to her side. Her stomach stirred as he kissed it, then helped her up as he stood himself, Evan getting to his feet on her other side.

In a daze, she pulled her clothes on in the dark, then sat by Evan at the table. Chad leaned against her desk, watching her, she found when she met his eyes.

She glanced to Evan, who was also looking at her, and flashed a quick smile in response to his crooked one. She found she had no idea what to say, but perhaps she didn't need to.

Eventually, she stood up, another breathless giggle escaping her as she spoke.

"I guess I'd better let you two head out." Quiet as it was, her voice sounded stark in the dark room. "You have a game to rest up for tomorrow." A wicked grin crossed her face as she felt a fluttering anticipation. She hadn't looked forward to watching a game this much in a long time.

"That we do. Will you be coming?" Evan asked. His impish smile suggested the entendre was intentional, even as his eyes reflected their usual innocence.

"Of course she will." Chad's voice was soft, but Rita's pussy jumped at its underlying commanding tone as he pushed away from the desk. He paused to let her walk in front of him, then continued, "And I'm sure we both look forward to seeing you." She felt the warmth of his body behind her as he whispered in her ear, "Out from under the bleachers this time."

Rita's breath caught. She started to turn around, but Chad's gentle hands landed on her hips and guided her forward as Evan reached to open the door for her. She let out a breath and turned to brush a kiss across Evan's lips as she nearly floated over the threshold.

It occurred to her she may want to rest up herself.

MONOCOQUE

VANESSA WU

M o n o c o q u e

He was not very tall. I guess he was about five foot six. But he was very slim and he eased himself into the seat beside me like a Formula One driver sinking down into his cockpit. The image came to my mind because he looked a bit like one of the drivers I'd recently seen on television in the build up to the Chinese Grand Prix. He was ruggedly handsome, with a strong jaw and a cleft chin. He looked like he'd just got out of bed because his brown hair was all tousled and wispy. He had a keen, impudent look in his eye as if there was nothing he wouldn't do.

We were on a plane at Heathrow airport preparing for a night flight to Shanghai.

"If we're going to spend ten hours together," he said. "I'm going to be pushing past you a lot."

That seemed like a delicious prospect. "I don't mind," I said. "I prefer to have the aisle seat. Just let me know when you want to squeeze by."

"I would have preferred an aisle seat," he said, "but I didn't know the procedure. I left it too late. I only reserved my seat at the last minute at the airport." He had a thick Swiss-German accent, like a farmer.

"Why didn't you do it online?"

"I've never flown before. I didn't know."

"But you're not English."

"No, I'm from Switzerland. I had to come via London for the flight to Shanghai."

I knew Switzerland well, having lived in Germany near the Swiss border for several years. We started chatting and I discovered he was from Bern. Bern people are well known for being ponderous and slow. I hoped he wasn't like that.

"How come you've never flown before?"

"Because I've never been outside Switzerland before."

"Really? Is that possible?"

"It's not only possible, it's a fact."

"I'm amazed."

"That's my first mission done, then."

"What mission?"

"As soon as I saw you, I made a mental note that I wanted to amaze you."

"Really? Why?"

He shrugged. "Is that a really stupid thing to say?"

"I hope not," I said.

"I'm not good at flirting with beautiful women."

"I don't mind if you want to practice," I said.

"And you are a very beautiful woman."

"Well, you are off to a good start," I said. "And it didn't take you long."

"I can be very quick."

Not a typical Bern man, then, I thought. I was pleased and flattered but I've learned not to be too encouraging around handsome men. "Your girlfriend should have told you that being quick is not necessarily a recommendation in a man," I said.

"It is if you have a passion for Formula One. I do. And that's why I don't have a girlfriend."

"Formula One?"

"That's my second mission."

"What is?"

"To see the race in Shanghai. That's why I decided to leave Switzerland finally. I'm a Formula One fan and I've got a ticket for the race in Shanghai."

"Why not choose a race closer to home?"

"Oh, I'll be going to some European races too. This is my year for adventures."

This is very promising, I thought. Then I said, truthfully, "You look a bit like a driver I saw on television."

"Which one?"

"I don't know his name. I didn't pay much attention. I don't understand motor racing. But I understood what he was saying very well because—oh, perhaps I'd better not say."

"No, go on, say it. What?"

"He said cars are like women and he's slept with

many beautiful women. But the trouble is, no matter how good looking a woman is, there's always a pimple on her bum."

"Really, did he say that?"

"Word for word, a pimple on her bum. Really! Like he's Mr. Perfect or something."

"Which driver was it?"

"I told you, I don't know."

"I'd never kick a girl out of bed for a pimple on her bum."

"No, I'd hope not," I said. Then I felt myself blushing in case he jumped to the wrong conclusions.

"You don't have a pimple on your bum, do you?" he asked.

"That's for me to know," I said, rather more harshly than I intended.

"Well, I wouldn't kick you out if you did," he said.

Actually he was more than handsome. I liked his lean physique. He was muscular without being brawny. He seemed very intelligent and I have a thing for intelligent men. The fact that he liked Formula One counted against him. It was not a sport I cared anything for. It seemed full of vain and superficial people who prized looks above substance. But I could easily drop my prejudices in the face of his warm, physical presence and his seductive gaze. I could drop more than my prejudices in fact. He was exactly the kind of man I could drop everything for, so when he talked of not kicking me out of bed I blushed again and felt very foolish and confused.

I covered my embarrassment with some polite phrases and busied myself with arranging my blanket and headphones while he talked nonsense about this and that. I wasn't really listening. I was registering his voice as a physical thing only, like fingers caressing my cheek or the wind in my hair. I had no idea of the meaning carried by his breath.

Then, as the stewardesses in the aisles adopted that stiff position that they always take just before they go through the safety instructions, his voice trailed off and was silent.

I was aware of him leaning towards me slightly, craning his neck to get a better look at the stewardesses. I think perhaps that was the moment that my desire for him became more than a passing fancy. It became a craving. It was sweet and delicious at first. I breathed in his scent. I willed his body to move closer to mine and I sensed my physical presence drawing him like a magnet. I imagined him without his shirt. I wanted to touch his skin.

But gradually, during the course of the flight, my craving grew and I began to feel pain. I wanted him. My body wanted him. It was a mono—mono—

"Monocoque," he said.

I blushed. "What?"

It was later in the flight. We had eaten a meal and I thought he had stopped talking for a while. He had been confusing me with technical babble I could scarcely follow. My mind had been wandering. But now he broke into my drifting thoughts with his strange Swiss-German accent uttering strange Frenchified words.

"The driver sits in a carbon fiber survival cell molded as a single shell," he was saying. "It's built to absorb the colossal energy of an impact, which is why you so often see a driver simply walk away from a crash."

"So there's no danger, then?" I said, knowing nothing about it. Whenever he talked of Formula One I would simply stare at his lips.

"Oh no, there's a lot of danger," he said, "But most of the time it's invisible. The danger comes from the G-forces. During a race the drivers have to withstand colossal G-forces similar to fighter pilots, only laterally instead of vertically. During cornering they might have to withstand forces up to four times the weight of their bodies, pressing against their ribs and neck. That can make it hard to breathe, so they have to be incredibly fit. You can black out if you're not prepared for it. But that's the drama you don't see, all that physical drama inside the cockpit."

"I think I prefer drama I can see," I said.

"But it's like anything," he said. "The more you know about it, the more interesting it gets." For some reason he was talking very quietly, almost whispering.

"I'm not a technical person."

"You don't need to be. You just need imagination. To be there, to feel what he is feeling, to get into his skin inside the monocoque."

My own skin tingled at his words, or was it at his eyes, which were gazing into mine with unholy zeal, willing me to understand him. His face was very close to mine. If it were any closer, I thought, we would be kissing.

"You take it very seriously," I said.

"I told you. It's a passion."

"That I can respect," I said.

And then they dimmed the lights.

"What is your name?" I asked him in the darkness.

"Torsten."

I touched his arm. "Good night, Torsten."

It felt good to touch his arm. I settled under my blanket and reclined my seat. Torsten did the same. Torsten. I knew his name now. I closed my eyes and let my head drift slowly towards his shoulder. It was warm and solid. I felt very safe. My desire grew stronger.

I will not try and tell you what agonies I suffered during the long hours of darkness huddled next to him—the discomfort ... the anxiety ... the fear of disturbing him ... my unceasing awareness of his body next to mine.

Perhaps I slept a little. But it was a troubled, frustrating sleep, full of unformed yearnings. I was hot between my thighs. No doubt I was wet. If I wasn't, I should have been. My body ached for him. I wanted to rest my hand on the flat of his stomach. I wanted his tongue inside me.

After the lights had come back on and the stewardesses were busying themselves with our breakfasts, I showed him an app on my phone that my friends in China used when they were chatting with me. "Let me add you," I said. "Then we can chat while you're in Shanghai."

"Don't I need that app too?"

"Sure, but it's free to download."

"I'll try it when I get to the hotel."

I passed him my phone so he could add himself to my contacts. Then when he downloaded the app, I would know.

I watched his fingers move across the screen as he tapped in the letters of his name. "What will you call yourself?" I said.

"How about Torsten?"

"There must be millions of Torstens."

"In China?"

"What about F1 Geek? I suggested."

"Doesn't it have to be one word?"

"I don't know."

"I'm useless at finding words," he said.

"What about that word you said when we were talking back there."

"What word?"

"Mono-something."

"Monocoque?"

"Yes. Monocoque. Tell me what it means again."

"It means a single shell."

"I see." Something else came to my mind. "Anyhow, call yourself Monocoque. And then, whenever I hear from you, I'll know to brace myself."

"Oh, I'll be gentle," he said.

"Not too gentle, I hope."

His eyes searched mine. I remembered that he'd never been outside Switzerland. Perhaps he'd never come across a woman like me. "G-forces are not entirely unwelcome," I explained.

He understood my meaning clearly enough then. I know because I saw him blush.

I'm not sure if I can say in all honesty that during the course of that flight I had become an expert in Formula One, but certainly my mind was racing. I was thinking of all the exciting adventures that Torsten might have and I very much wanted to be one of them. I can't remember all the details of what he told me but I can remember with complete accuracy the mercurial motion of his lips and the hypnotic stillness of his eyes. And then we landed and there was the tedious routine of passport control, baggage collection, currency exchange and onward transportation.

Traveling is a string of small trials.

Torsten didn't seem too distressed by them. Perhaps he could learn to like traveling as much as I had learned to like Formula One. As we passed through customs and into the departure area I felt a pang of separation. "Keep in touch," I told him, making a meaningful gesture at my phone. Then I watched him head towards the bus stop that would take him towards Jiading district, while I headed towards the center of Shanghai.

Strangely, it was still morning. Thursday. Luckily, when I arrived at my hotel they were able to let me into my room and I freshened up again. I was supposed to have a meeting in the afternoon. Then on Friday there would be more meetings. In the world of Formula One, I had learned, Friday and Saturday were practice days and on Sunday there was the race. But in my world it would be meetings, meetings, meetings, with many notes to take and reports to prepare. If I was going to see Torsten again, I needed to act quickly. He had told me he would be leaving again right after the race. That didn't give me much time. I needed to get tickets to the race. I had no idea how to do it but I had a cousin in the government. Maybe he knew.

I phoned him immediately. That first call was very long. There were many formalities and courtesies to get through. My cousin didn't know anything about the race but he gave me the number of a high-ranking party official who might be able to help. The official gave me another number of a Mr. Zhang and this time I got lucky.

"You want tickets to the race?" Mr. Zhang asked me suspiciously.

"One ticket, that's all."

"They are hard to get, you know."

"I know but I'm desperate."

His voice became interested. "How desperate?"

I took a deep breath. I have dealt with Chinese officials before. It's never good to be beholden to them. "Incredibly desperate," I said. "I'll do anything."

There was a long pause. I could hear him thinking. I knew he was still there because the line was hushed, like a grand empty stateroom that reeked of power.

"I need to see a photograph," he said at last. "Text me a photograph of yourself. If you look suitable I will call you back."

I took a picture on my phone and sent it to him.

Silence.

I waited for four, five minutes. My heart felt like it would leap through my rib cage. I was crushed by invisible G-forces more terrible than anything on a racetrack.

Then my phone purred.

I struggled to answer it with fumbling fingers.

"I am arranging an event for some F1 dignitaries on Saturday evening," Mr. Zhang said. "But it's very select. I could arrange for you to get an entrance."

"No, I don't want that. I want to get into the race!"

"If you get into this event, you will get into the race," he said calmly. His words were so soft, so smooth, so certain that I never doubted him for an instant.

"Very well. But how?"

"Do you have a pen?"

I scrabbled in my bag for a pen, excitement mounting.

"I'm going to give you an address. I want you to meet me there at six in the evening on Saturday. Can you do that?"

"Yes, yes! Where?"

"You must come alone."

"I will. Give me the address!"

"You must come alone and don't worry about what to wear. If I like you, I will provide some clothes."

He told me the address then, quickly. So quickly that

I didn't have time to think. As soon as I finished writing, he hung up. I looked at the address but I was thinking about his words. Clothes?

What kind of clothes?

But there was no more time to think. I would have liked to sleep, but I supposed it was better to keep myself occupied and sleep at a more appropriate hour. I changed into a business suit and set off for my first meeting in Pudong, the financial district of Shanghai.

I lost the next day to jet lag. I was miserable. Torsten hadn't called me and I was in a state of nervous tension in which my emotions felt taut and brittle. The least thing was likely to make me cry. I had several business meetings in which I was trying desperately hard to focus and in one of them I had to leave the room and go to the toilet and wipe the dirt of Shanghai from my eyes.

I returned to my room at about eight o'clock, shattered. I had been checking my phone all day for signs of Torsten but there had been none. I had clearly made less of an impression on him than he had made on me. Disappointment clouded my thoughts. I had been so sure that there'd been a connection between us, the promise of something more than friendship. It was hard to learn that I'd been wrong. I could hardly accept it. But I had no time for self-pity. I had to keep pushing myself onwards, forcing myself to function.

I tossed my clothes onto the bed, had a shower and wrapped myself in a towel. I was too tired even to dry myself properly. I dabbed at my damp skin as if it were bruised.

Then I saw it. A blue bubble had popped up on my phone. Monocoque!

Monocoque: Hi.

Van_wu: Hiya!!!

I sent him a rabbit dancing amid flowers.

Monocoque: Busy?

Van_wu: Finished for the day.

Monocoque: Give yourself a pat on the back.

Van_wu: Just a shower and sleep will do.

Monocoque: Don't let me keep you from your shower.

Van_wu: I've already had it.

Monocoque: Damn! I missed it.

Van_wu: You can catch the sequel.

Monocoque: Even better.

Van_wu: I'm still damp.

Monocoque: Damp or wet?

Van_wu: Getting wetter.

Yes, I'm ashamed to reveal that I went straight to the point. It had been a long day. I sent him a sashaying kitten.

Monocoque: Are you naked?

Van_wu: Yes, under this towel.

Monocoque: Take it off.

Van_wu: In a while.

Monocoque: Send a pic.

No more pics today, I thought. I wanted something for myself. I'd become desperately horny within seconds of seeing the word *Monocoque* on my phone. All my cares fell away and I just wanted to touch myself.

Van_wu: You'll see me in the flesh soon enough.

Monocoque: How?

Van_wu: I'm coming to the race.

Monocoque: On Sunday?

Van_wu: Yes.

Monocoque: Cool. How did you get a ticket?

Van_wu: Connections.

Monocoque: I still need a pic.

I hesitate to give you the verbatim transcript that followed. The trouble with text is that it tells only a part of the story. It can't convey the build up of anguish and desire during the day. It can't show you the nerves I felt at saying anything sexual at all to this stranger whom I'd met on the plane; or explain why a mere stranger had gotten under my skin and infected me with sudden passion. A few crude words of text can look dirty on the page. No doubt my words were crude and dirty. But his were a thing of exquisite beauty to me, flooding me with relief. My sexual feelings surged out and I had no qualms about expressing them to him.

Van_wu: Would it make you hard if I sent you a pic?

Monocoque: I'm already hard.

Van_wu: What made you hard?

Monocoque: Thinking about you in that towel.

Van_wu: I'm no longer in it.

Monocoque: *Gulp!*

Van_wu: I am draped on the bed on my back.

Monocoque: *Gasp!*

Van_wu: Tell me what you want.

Monocoque: I want you.

Van_wu: What would you do with me?

Monocoque: Fuck the hell out of you.

Van_wu: Yes please.

Monocoque: I need to see between your thighs.

Van_wu: Is that what you are thinking about?

Monocoque: Always.

Van_wu: Did you think about it before?

Monocoque: Of course.

Van_wu: Did you think about it on the plane?

Monocoque: I kept looking at you when you were sleeping.

Van_wu: Really?

Monocoque: But not down there.

Van_wu: But you wanted to?

Monocoque: Oh, I so wanted to!

Van_wu: I would have let you. You could have touched me.

Monocoque: Next time!

Van_wu: I was thinking about your cock.

Monocoque: Did you want to see it?

Van_wu: I wanted to suck it.

Monocoque: Oh!

Van_wu: I wish I could suck it now.

Monocoque: My hotel is too far away.

Van_wu: I know. I'll have to wait.

Monocoque: You know after the race I have to catch a flight.

Van_wu: I know.

Monocoque: So how are we going to meet?

Van_wu: I am coming to the race.

Monocoque: Are you going to suck my cock there?

Van_wu: Maybe.

Monocoque: You would really suck my cock at the race?

Van_wu: And more.

Monocoque: What more is there?

Van_wu: I want you inside me.

Monocoque: ...

Van_wu: Are you there?

Monocoque: ...

Van_wu: What are you doing?

Monocoque: ...

Van_wu: Tell me you are thinking about putting your cock inside me.

Monocoque: I am.

Van_wu: I am so wet from thinking about it.

Monocoque: ...

Van_wu: Can you imagine what it would feel like to put the full length of your cock inside me?

Monocoque: ...

Van_wu: I am so slick, so tight. I would grip you and squeeeeeze you.

Monocoque: I know you would.

Van_wu: Maybe bending over, squinting through the fence at one of those tight hairpins.

Monocoque: ...

Van_wu: I'm going to wear my shortest skirt …

Monocoque: …

Van_wu: and maybe a thong or some very skimpy panties, or nothing at all, so that when I bend over you can see

Van_wu: everything.

Van_wu: You could just come up to me from behind and put your hand right up against my

Van_wu: pussy and feel how wet I am then you could press your

Van_wu: hard cock against my pussy lips you would find my hole and feel

Van_wu: how tight it is inside me so very tight but wet because of you and what you do to me.

Monocoque: …

Van_wu: Would you like that?

Monocoque: …

Van_wu: What's happening?

Monocoque: You made me come.

Van_wu: So quick?

Monocoque: I told you I was quick.

Yes, it was quick. *He* was quick. He had come while I was just beginning to warm to my theme. I was dissatisfied but I wasn't disappointed. I was still wet. I still wanted him. I was more determined than ever to see him again.

> **Van_wu:** I've got to see you for real.
>
> **Monocoque:** No, I've got to see you!
>
> **Van_wu:** When?
>
> **Monocoque:** Come to the practice tomorrow.
>
> **Van_wu:** I don't have a ticket yet.
>
> **Monocoque:** Damn!
>
> **Van_wu:** I will get it tomorrow and come on Sunday.
>
> **Monocoque:** What about Saturday night?
>
> **Van_wu:** Where will you be?
>
> **Monocoque:** In my hotel.

I knew that seeing him in his hotel room on Saturday would only give me a part of the whole. I would want to be with him all the next day. I would want to share his passion. I was more determined than ever to get a ticket to Sunday's race.

I lay back on the bed and covered myself. Yes, I had truly been naked and uncovered during our chat. It had excited me that I was lying there in that position while he was reading my words. I liked the fact that my thighs were spread wide and my pussy lips were pornographically parted. I had even been moving my hips and touching myself with a slippery finger. It excited me beyond words.

But it was only after he'd gone that the real physical

pleasure could begin, and for that I didn't need to be open or exposed. I could hide under the duvet and lie in darkness, for now it was just about me. The only stimulation I wanted was my imagination and my fingertips. The touch of the white cotton duvet against my bare skin was soothing and sensual. I felt sheltered and safe. I let myself go completely.

Afterwards I needed something more. Instead of turning onto my side and falling asleep like I normally do, I did something else. I turned on the light and took a picture. My face had turned pink. My throat too. The red bloom even covered the skin between my breasts. I took a picture of it. Then I sent the picture to Monocoque.

—◇◇◇◇—

The place where I had to meet Mr. Zhang was close to the municipal buildings in People's Square. I arrived a few minutes before six. I was expecting to be kept waiting but when I introduced myself to the concierge, he told me to go straight up to the twenty-second floor. A man in a dark gray suit was waiting by the elevator as I arrived.

"Mr. Zhang?"

"Yes. Follow me."

He led me to an office. There was not much in it, just a desk, two chairs, a couple of filing cabinets and a cupboard. On the desk was a large, flat cardboard box. The walls were pale gray. There were no pictures but there was a window that looked out onto People's Square, which gave the room an air of grandeur.

"You like the view?" he asked me, noticing the way I was staring at the clumps of trees far below in the center of the busy roadway. Surrounding the square were walls of skyscrapers, some of them brandishing corporate logos so that the park in the center of the square looked like a shrine to commerce.

"It's impressive," I said. "Is this your office?"

"For the moment," he said. Then he looked at me sharply. "Miss Wu, let us get to the point. You want a ticket for tomorrow's race?"

"Yes."

He stood in front of the sturdy wooden desk and eyed me critically. He appraised me from head to toe and there was a half smile on his lips that made me nervous. He knew he held all the power in the room. He came towards me. "What made you wear a business suit?" He touched the lapel of my jacket and ran his fingers up and down it as if judging the quality of the cloth.

"I'm in Shanghai on business," I said. "I've had meetings all day."

"So now you are ready to relax?"

"Tomorrow I will be. If you can help me."

"I think I can help you." His hand hadn't left my jacket. Now it pressed closer to me so that I could feel the warmth from his fingers against my breast.

Immediately I stepped back. "My cousin knows I am here," I said.

"I was only admiring your suit," he said and his voice

was soft and ingratiating.

I met his eyes without blinking. I was aware of the position I'd put myself in. I wasn't under any illusions.

He approached again and this time I stopped him with a gesture. "Come no further," I said. "Let's get to the point. The ticket."

"I need you to attend an event this evening. I will take you there. Then you will get your ticket."

"I have plans for this evening."

"You must change them," he said.

He took a step towards me. I held up a hand. "No closer!"

"Your perfume is gorgeous," he said. "It's filling the room."

"My perfume is not so strong."

"Something is making me dizzy," he insisted.

"Loosen your collar," I told him. "You look hot."

He loosened his tie and undid the top button of his shirt. His fingers were delicate, like an artist's. His eyes remained fixed on me all the while.

"I'm always suspicious of a man who wears a suit and tie on a Saturday," I said.

"I have prestigious clients to impress."

"And you want me to help you with this?"

"Beautiful women always help business to run smoothly, especially in Formula One."

"How late would I have to stay at this event?" I was feeling torn. The point of getting the ticket was to be with

Torsten. I could bear much for the sake of being with him. But how much? If I could go to Mr. Zhang's event and still see Torsten afterwards, we would all be satisfied.

"You can leave whenever you wish."

"Where is this event?"

"Jiading District."

"Near the motor racing track?"

"Very near." While I was thinking about this I must have dropped my guard. In a flash he was behind me and his swift hands were relieving me of my jacket.

"What are you doing?"

"You are going to get changed. I have something I want you to wear."

I let him pull my arms out the sleeves. He laid the jacket down on the desk. He moved the cardboard box aside as he did so and I realized that what he wanted me to wear must be inside the box. But he didn't open it. Instead he came back to me and stared at my chest as if his eyes were trying to pop open the buttons.

I pointed to behind the desk. "You stand on that side of the desk," I said.

His complexion had turned very pink. He seemed to be wrestling with some kind of inner tumult.

"You must get undressed," he said.

"Is what you want me to wear inside that box?"

"It is."

"Then move aside. Stand behind the desk and open it."

He stood his ground a moment, staring at me. "That perfume," he murmured.

"My perfume is very light."

He loosened his tie some more and, with a swiftness that surprised me, was suddenly behind the desk and lifting the lid of the box.

Inside was a Red Army military uniform. He lifted out the jacket to show me. It was vintage, not the latest design. There was a star on each shoulder.

"What rank is that?"

"Second lieutenant."

"Only second? Can't I be first?"

"This is from 1963. Any earlier and you would have no rank at all."

The trousers had a wide red stripe down the side. He had even acquired a green peaked cap with a red star on it.

"Are we going to some sort of military parade?"

"Western men have this little fantasy," he said. "They want to be waited on by a cute Chinese girl in military uniform."

"So you want me to be a waitress?"

"Oh, you don't need to do any work," he said. "You just need to look beautiful, which you do, I can assure you, without any effort at all."

"How did you know my size?"

"Is it your size?"

"I don't know."

"Put it on," he urged gently. "Let's find out."

Mr Zhang stayed obediently on his side of the desk while I changed out of my clothes and into the thin cotton uniform. The fit wasn't perfect but it was close enough. Tightening the belt on the trousers I looked across at him and asked him what he thought.

He was biting his lower lip.

"Are you all right?"

He was leaning forward with his palms flat on the surface of the desk. He appeared to be in pain. "That—look—is—perfect!" he managed to say before suddenly moving back from the edge of the desk and covering his groin with those delicate, artistic hands of his.

"I need a moment," he said apologetically. "I must spend a moment in the restroom before we set off."

"Take your time."

He disappeared down the corridor for a few moments. When he came back he was much more relaxed, and I did not question him. "Ready to go?" he asked me.

I gathered up the cardboard box, which now contained my own clothes. "May I bring this?"

"Of course. We can put it in a locker for you until you are ready to leave."

"Will there be other women in uniform at this event?"

"That is the idea."

"I'm feeling strangely nervous," I said.

"No need to be. There won't be anyone as beautiful as you."

"Your flattery is far too exaggerated. What about the

men?"

"You will find them handsome enough."

"Which men are they?"

"No names," he said. He wagged his finger expressively. "Strictly, no names."

———◇◇◇◇———

The Jiading International Circuit looks like something dropped from another galaxy. Mr. Zhang took me there in a quiet black Mercedes driven by his personal chauffeur. I held my breath as we entered the road leading into the circuit. The scale and sweep of the architecture overawed me. I felt humbled and dwarfed by it. A hushed, almost holy, feeling came over me. There was an unearthly stillness and silence upon the place. I became conscious of the steady whirr of the car's climate control for the first time.

"So where we are going is actually in the circuit?" I asked Mr. Zhang.

"Yes. I promised you, didn't I?"

"You promised me a ticket for the race."

"You will get your ticket," he insisted.

The car pulled up in a parking lot ringed with security fences. From there, we were taken by an electric buggy to a huge glass and steel structure overlooking the race track.

"Over there are the pits," said Mr. Zhang, pointing to a row of garages to our right. "This is a high security area. Wear this." He gave me a VIP pass on a lanyard. "Put it over your head," he said.

I followed him into the towering building. I saw it was one of a pair. Then we were in an elevator going up.

We got out on the top floor where there were several women in the reception area. They were all Chinese, slightly taller than me, with long legs and almond-shaped faces. They were dressed like me in army green with red facings to their uniforms. Two of them wore knee-high leather boots in the same shade as their wide leather belts. They were sitting or standing by the reception desk and were obviously escorts. One of them carried a whip.

Mr. Zhang spoke to them as if he knew them. They looked at me more than him, appraising me from head to toe just as Mr. Zhang had done earlier. Then one of them pointed to a door and told him the key code.

"You can take off your VIP pass," he said. "But keep it safe. You will need it for the race tomorrow. Leave your things here. The girls will put them in a locker for you. Collect them when you leave."

I did as he said then followed him to an opaque chrome door. He punched in the numbers and we went into a large room furnished in luxurious style. Some old Chinese pop songs were playing softly in the background. There were about thirty people in the room. If I'd known then what I know now about Formula One, I expect I would have recognized some of them. But of course I still couldn't have given you names. I have been sworn to secrecy. All I can tell you is that the people smelled of money.

"I will leave you now," he said. "Do your best to

blend in." My heart began beating frenetically. He gave me a last look, up and down. His soft brown eyes seemed sad and affectionate. He leaned over and gently unfastened the top two buttons of my tunic. I swear he must have felt my heart leaping up against his fingers. Then his lips brushed my cheek and he was gone.

If I hadn't wanted that ticket so badly I might have turned and followed him. I felt very nervous. But before my fear could dominate me a man grasped my hand and led me into the room. He babbled away about something and I answered his questions without paying much attention to what I said. The room was partly in shadow. He led me further into the room and towards a door at the far end where the shadows were deepest.

"Let's find some privacy," he said.

We went through the door into a small room furnished with a plush red sofa and lit by flickering candles.

A woman was seated on the sofa. "Hi!" she said. "I'm Lulu."

She had the almond-shaped face of a classical Chinese beauty. Her hair was tied back and away from her face so that it could be seen in all its perfection. Even though she was seated, I could tell that her legs were long. She shifted them to the side graciously, as though inviting me to sit down beside her.

I introduced myself.

"You seem nervous, Vanessa. Are you scared of me or what?"

"Perhaps she is scared of *me*." A man had approached at that moment and introduced himself as Jay. His accent was foreign but I couldn't place it. I didn't reply because I was wondering if he meant "Jay" the name or "J" the initial.

"Cat got your tongue?" he said.

"Sorry," I said. "I—"

Lulu's army tunic was fastened loosely with her leather belt. She shifted her position and I suddenly noticed that she was naked underneath.

"Sit down," she said in a soft, tremolo voice. "I don't bite."

"What were you expecting?" asked Jay. He was standing close behind me and his arm snaked out and touched me lightly across my back. I twisted to look at him. He was astonishingly good looking. He had clear blue eyes that studied my face intelligently.

"Not this," I said.

"Did you think you were coming to an orgy or something?" he asked.

"Yes. Or something."

"But surely, this is much nicer, isn't it?"

He put his hands on my shoulders and pressed me down gently onto the sofa. Then he sat between us. His hand had somehow found its way to my thigh and he was caressing it.

"So, are you a sergeant, a sergeant major or a lieutenant?" he asked me.

"I'm whatever you want me to be," I said.

"I knew from the moment I saw that you were already exactly what I wanted. You are very beautiful," he said, studying my eyes.

"Thank you."

"Is your body as lovely as your face?"

"I think it is not as lovely as Lulu's."

Jay looked at each of us in turn. "Oh, I don't know," he said. "Perhaps only the most thorough and scrupulous analysis can tell. Lulu is certainly one of the most beautiful women I have ever seen."

"Ha-ha. You are both audacious flatterers," said Lulu, showing her beautiful open mouth. Her lips were so sensual I couldn't help staring at them.

"I am not flattering," Jay said. "It's the truth. You aren't going to punish me for speaking the truth, are you?"

"All men should be punished," said Lulu in that seductive, little-girl voice of hers.

"Oh, no," I said. "Or, at least, if they are punished, it should only be for the benefit of women."

Jay laughed. He really had the most seductive blue eyes, with a playful gleam in them. "How can a man's punishment benefit you?" he asked me.

"Men are so quick to pounce on women," I said. "Look at the way you grabbed me as I came into the room. But what I would like to see is a man who is made to stick at his task until a woman is satisfied."

"You would like to see that, would you?" he asked me. His tone suggested I was nothing but a dirty voyeur.

"I've no objection," purred Lulu.

"You too?" he asked her. "The two of you would punish me by keeping me in heaven?"

"You are all talk," said Lulu.

He took the cue, opened his mouth a little and moved in on Lulu for a lingering kiss.

I have said that I'm irritated by the cult of beauty in Formula One. It is a ridiculously superficial world. Yet, as those two exquisitely beautiful people entwined together in erotic harmony, I could see the value in superficiality. Their faces were bewitching. Their skin was pure. Their bodies were luscious. But it was their eyes that turned me on. Lust gleamed darkly there, vivid and uncompromising. I was mesmerized by it.

Jay's hand slipped inside Lulu's tunic with an ease of movement that went almost unnoticed until I noticed that he had bared her breast, squeezing and tweaking the perky, mauve nipple until it puckered up beneath his touch. Its responsiveness made him cry out with joy and desire, his tongue touched his top lip and he twitched as if surprised by an electric shock.

She was beautiful!

The plump, velvety softness of her breast contrasted gorgeously with the manly roughness of his face as he bent forward for a closer look and planted a full-lipped kiss inside her clothes. He ripped open her tunic and her breasts bounced, taut and inviting, as her nipples stood up bold and clear beside his whiskers. His lips fastened upon one proud little nub and he sucked ferociously. Again, I watched her eyes. How can I describe the expression of pleasure and anticipation in them? She was in the fulfillment of a dream. She was ready to do anything, in thrall and liberated at the same time, on the brink of ecstasy.

Jay's strong, sure hands slid over her hips and found her bottom. He caressed it with obvious pleasure. The smooth curve of it beneath her tight army trousers was simply magnificent and Jay's hand swept along the contours with masterful authority. He squeezed and stroked. He was in control and she submitted joyfully.

I could see his tongue anticipating the next phase. His eyes smoldered with lust. In a flash he had turned her over so that she was kneeling on the sofa and he had unfastened those tight military trousers to bare her gorgeous flesh.

Her skin was flawless. Yes. There was not a single blemish. And I saw everything. Everything.

She was wearing a pale silk thong. It was almost transparent and was so light and flimsy that it was hardly there at all. Jay pressed his whiskered cheeks right up against the soft arc of her bottom and slurped with his eager tongue at the wispy fabric. Her body responded. She was his.

It was the strangest voyeuristic experience I have ever had. Her rear end was raised up towards me and I could see his stubbled chin nestled between her legs. He pressed his tongue flat against her flesh, not on her pussy but next to it, right between her legs. His fingers clutched at her buttocks and created white, colorless streaks in the creamy flesh. I think

I will never see such a spotless behind so close again. When he let go of her and his fine, skillful hands rested casually on her hips, her buttocks reverted to a shape of sublime and sensual beauty.

The thong came away. I don't know how. It disappeared before my eyes. Her bottom was raised up towards the ceiling and her long legs were tucked in so that Jay was leaning over her upturned rear end. He parted her flesh and probed with his long, broad tongue. Lulu's face turned pink. She bit her bottom lip and moaned. Such a moan! And Jay's tongue wasn't done yet. He licked with utter lust and probed further until his tongue entered her, moving with phenomenal speed and strength.

Lulu was so near to orgasm, but Jay wasn't yet ready to let her.

He turned her over again and presented me with another view of the planes, slopes and angles of her naked body. Then he took off his shirt. He had the taut, muscular beauty of a professional athlete, slim and small but very strong. His skin, like hers, had a freshness to it that was close to miraculous. Here and there it was covered in soft, beautiful hair that glowed in the candlelight.

They rearranged themselves on the sofa once again. Lulu wanted to get at his underwear. She pulled down his trousers to reveal tight cotton bulging with manly promise. Her rear end was towards my face again, and I peered round her bottom to watch as she peeled back Jay's briefs. His cock sprang out, erect and ready, and her mouth closed over it.

His lower body disappeared under a veil of shiny black hair. Then I noticed the wetness seeping from Lulu's pussy. She was very aroused. She raised and lowered her hips as her head worked on his cock, and I noticed the dark protrusion of her inner lips slick with her juices. I was surprised by the transparency of the liquid and I stared for a moment or two, wanting almost to touch it but unsure if my touch would be welcome. Desire rose within me as my own fingers, so deprived of sensation, began to touch myself.

But I wasn't given the chance to be a passive spectator for long. Once again they shifted position. Now Lulu was on her back with her head in my lap, her glossy hair spread out like a fan. I looked down the length of her body at Jay, who was positioning himself for entry. Heaving her calves up onto his shoulders, he lunged forward and his fine, fiery cock was swallowed up inside her. I could feel her body tightening and tensing as she drew him in and gripped him. Her exhalations of pleasure were very loud in the small room. Their two bodies moved as one.

I held her shoulders, marveling at the softness of her skin as he thrust inside her, his own moans low and urgent, his eyes lost.

Lost.

That's how I felt too. Lost in this spectacle of ecstasy. It was like being on another planet. My little world dropped away from me and I was transported to a place and time that I will never find again.

Quite how long the three of us remained locked

together in this act of passion, I don't know. Time was meaningless. I just know that my heart was pounding against my ribs and the pressure of Lulu's head against my groin was gradually pushing me towards my own inevitable orgasm. I was engulfed by the hot scent of their lust. I was hypnotized by their rhythm, by their murmurings and by the dreamy intensity in their eyes.

Lulu came and I felt her pleasure ripple through me. Her neck became hot as I caressed her cheek and shoulder. Jay was inside her and I saw his whole body suddenly stiffen. His eyes rolled in his head. Oh! I could almost feel his seed shoot through her. Their shared pleasure was like an electric haze into which I was helplessly drawn.

I forced myself to get out from under them. I was there for a purpose and I was determined not to lose sight of my mission.

"Excuse me one moment," I said as I eased myself free. I made quickly for the exit and rejoined the four sexy girls in the reception area.

I was breathless with nervous excitement. "I was told I could get a ticket for the race tomorrow," I said.

"Yes. Didn't you have it when you came in?"

"What? No."

"Yes. I put it in the locker for you." She went to the locker and fetched my things. "Here," she said, handing me the VIP badge on the lanyard. "This pass. That's your entry for the race. You can use it all weekend."

I looked at the pass and sure enough it said ADMIT

ONE with the dates for Friday, Saturday and Sunday.

"Can I call a taxi?" I asked her.

"Sure. There are several waiting below. I'll call down to one and tell him to take you wherever you want to go."

Fifteen minutes later I was at Torsten's hotel.

"Vanessa!"

"Not too late am I?"

"You are not late at all, but why are you wearing that uniform?"

"Weird story," I said pushing past him into his room. "I'll explain a little later."

He shut the door and looked me up and down with an expression of disbelief.

"Well, aren't you at least going to kiss me?" I asked him.

He approached and put his hand on my waist. "You're hot."

"I'm a little out of breath. It was a rush getting here."

He was distracted by the leather belt. "Where did you get this?" he asked me.

I tossed the cap on his bed and shook out my hair. "Family friend—sort of. Do you like it?" I came closer and hugged him. "Oh my god, you're hard. What were you doing, watching porn?"

"No. It's the uniform. You look so sexy."

He looked sexy too. He was dressed very casually in crumpled linen trousers and a T-shirt but he wore them with style. He had an unselfconscious grace. I liked the way he held his upper body. He was muscled under his T-shirt. I could make out the firm lines of his pecs.

I put my arms around his warm body and he drew me close.

"Oh my god, you smell good."

"Do I?"

He put his hands through my hair. "What is that perfume called?"

"Just kiss me!" I said.

He put his lips on mine and we kissed. It was the first time. It seemed hardly possible but it was true. His hard cock was against my thigh and his hands were exploring the fabric of my uniform. His tongue tasted sweet.

His hand slipped inside my trousers and he touched me between my legs. His fingers rubbed gently at my pussy. The scene I'd witnessed at the racetrack had made me very aroused and Torsten's fingers discovered my secret.

"You're already wet."

"You got there faster than I expected," I said.

"I'm just seeing if you're ready."

"Oh, I'm ready," I said. "But please don't be quick!"

We moved to the bed. "Your skin is so soft. Doesn't the uniform itch?"

"No. Did you want me to keep it on?"

"I would rather see all of you." He peeled back the tunic and grasped my breasts through my bra. His fingers found my nipples. I squirmed as he touched them. I wanted him so badly.

He reached behind me and unhooked my bra. He tried to kiss my breasts but I wouldn't allow it. Instead I pushed him down onto the bed and unbuttoned his shirt. He had a fine, flat stomach and the toned limbs of someone who exercises regularly.

He lay there open-mouthed while I hovered above him, running my fingers down his body. He was trying to catch one of my breasts in his mouth but he couldn't. I was on top of him, holding him with my weight. He could have thrown me off easily enough but he had become temporarily listless as if drugged by my perfume.

My fingers found the buttons on his trousers and worked quickly to unfasten them and pull them down.

"You are so forceful," he said.

"Because I want you," I told him.

He was wearing purple briefs with a broad, tight, elastic waistband. He was already in a state of total arousal, the tip of his cock peeking out of the top.

He moaned softly as I squeezed it between my thumb and forefinger.

"Are you sure you weren't watching porn?" I asked him.

"No porn was ever this good," he said.

I peeled back his briefs. His cock was so lovely that I wanted to kiss it. I could see it straining and wanting to be touched. I pulled off his underwear completely and made him wait, brushing my fingernails over his sensitive skin. I was tempted to suck his cock but it was so hard and eager that I kissed only his hips and groin. I touched around his penis and then held it tentatively. I wondered how much he could take before it would explode. The temptation to put my lips over it was overwhelming and in the end I couldn't resist. I licked the tip and took it very lightly between my lips. It was gorgeous. I could feel him extend into my mouth, his hips rising with eagerness. But I only licked softly around the surfaces, teasing him still.

"I want you inside me," I said. "But you have to make me come first."

"Get on top," he said. "So you control it." He suddenly flipped me off him, showing how strong he was. "But only after I've teased you like you've been teasing me."

He took one of my breasts and squeezed it into his gaping mouth. He sucked hard on it and clamped his lips down on my nipple as he drew his head back. " I can't tell you how I've longed to do that," he said. He found my other breast and sucked ferociously. His hands were on my bottom. He was digging into me with his fingers. "You've got such a shapely ass!" he said.

I let him undo the belt and take off my military trousers.

"Do I have any pimples?"

"Let me take a look!"

His hands went inside my panties and groped my flesh. I stood on the floor so I could remove my panties and he turned me so that my bottom was in his face. He squeezed and flattened his face against my buttocks, and I could feel his tongue slide between them. It felt strange and so very intimate. I could feel myself becoming wetter, electrified by the unusual sensation.

I let him take his pleasure for a while. I bent over and his fingers slipped inside me. He bit me gently and licked my skin. But I didn't want to be passive. I turned to face him. I really liked to look at his cock. We were both naked now. I touched his cock again and wet it with my mouth. Then I forced him back down on the bed and climbed on top of him.

Gently, I lowered myself onto him and we started to move in rhythm. We were facing one another. I reached behind and caressed his balls. I could feel his shaft right up inside me, very deep. He bucked a little but I controlled it from on top, keeping the rhythm slow and gentle. I even leaned back a little, wet my finger and touched it to my clit. His face was red and his eyes were wide and glazed. I started to massage my clit. He craned his neck so he could see and I felt him flex excitedly inside me.

That was quite intense. I could feel the cheeks of my ass pressing softly against his balls, his hips bucking fiercely and his cock plunging deep and fast. As much as I tried to control it, he was too strong for me. Too quick. I leaned forward and let him bite my breasts. He played with my nipples between his teeth. I wasn't sure which of us would come first, but I didn't want it to be this fast so I tried to get off him. This felt so deliciously good but eventually, reluctantly I pulled free.

I'd seen in Formula One that there are technicians in

the pit lane who hold up signs for the drivers as they hurtle past the pits. P1 means position one.

Now it was time to try P2.

"I like it when you bite my nipples," I said. "But do it softly."

He sat up and massaged my breasts and nipples. Then he let his tongue do the work. Gradually, naturally, he started to take more control until I found myself lying on my back being treated to the most glorious sucking kisses and nibbles.

I touched myself. "Oh my god, I'm so wet!"

"I perform very well in the wet," he said.

"I hope so!" I raised my legs into the air, and he ducked under them to line himself up. "Fast or slow, you decide," I said. "But go in deep."

I watched him in the mirror on the wall. He was perfect in profile. His body was lean, sleek and firm. His rhythm was steady. His thrusts were strong. I closed my eyes. It was heavenly. If I close my eyes now I can still remember a ghost of the sensations. But there is nothing like the real thing.

"Don't come! Don't come!" I screamed at him as his thrusts grew more and more powerful.

I was fearful because he was so frenetic. I thought surely he would spill his seed in me this time. But he soothed me with slow caresses and pulled out, still hard, still eager, ready for P3.

Now, my forearms were flat on the pillows and my

bottom in the air. Torsten grasped my hips and took full control. I wanted to twist round and look, but with my face buried in the pillows there was nothing I could do. He found my sweet spot and I was totally under his command. I couldn't even control the speed. He accelerated full on the throttle. My body buckled under unbearable forces. There were squeals, a sudden spurt and a final dramatic slide to the finish.

I didn't say anything for a while. But I was satisfied. I was more than satisfied.

After a long silence, Torsten was the first to speak. "I think we were neck and neck on the qualifying round," he said.

"You mean that was only the qualifying round?"

"The real thing is tomorrow," he said. "If you're still up for it."

"Oh, I'm up for it," I said. "But aren't there *two* qualifying rounds?"

He looked up and down the length of my naked body stretched on the bed beside him. "If you're on a hot lap, there are three ... and we don't have much time," he said.

I let my legs fall open. I wasn't sleepy. I touched myself and showed him how much I still wanted him. "We have all night," I said.

"Then I think we might just squeeze something in."

The best place to stand at the Jiading circuit is at the

entrance to turn 8, according to Torsten.

"The drivers are coming out of a fast left-hander and suddenly have to flick right. They are pulling about three G through the chicane and you can see how good a driver is from the angle of his head. Only the good ones can actually see where they are going."

I couldn't hear Torsten's explanations very well but I was happy to stand with him on the corner. He stood behind me, in fact, with his arms clasped around me, shouting in my ear. We both became more and more excited as the cars whizzed past. Their engines were ferocious. The vibrations went right through me and made my whole body feel like it was turning to goo. Or maybe it was the effect of Torsten's kisses at my ear and his sly hands between my legs under my skirt.

Torsten had certainly learned to vary his pace. I noticed that Formula One drivers had more to them than just speed, too. Yes, they were quick on the straight but they slowed almost to a standstill on the corners. Perfection is not about straight line speed but knowing when to brake, how to go gently, when to wait and when to push hard.

Torsten had all the qualities of a first rate driver. He touched me so lightly and deftly that nobody but me was aware of it. And yet his touch was firm and controlled and assertive. He touched exactly the right spot. Consistently. Expertly. Precisely. He brought me to a knee-bending, shuddering climax. And, for all the breathtaking beauty of the action on the plush red sofa, for all the night-long excitement on Torsten's bed, I know that the touch of his fingers under my skirt, as I watched the action on the track, will always be my most cherished memory of that trip to Shanghai. And a very beautiful consequence of that subtle finger play under my skirt was that I became a Formula One fan and bought tickets to the British Grand Prix. Torsten extended his newly-discovered passion for travel and met me that summer in Silverstone.

After two frenzied nights of lovemaking, he started to show signs of wear. He lay on his back staring at the ceiling while I toyed with the hairs on his chest.

"I'll let you have a little pit stop, then I want to try a different ride height," I said.

"Can't you see there's nothing left in the tank?"

"That's what the pit stop's for."

"You aren't allowed to refuel in the pit anymore."

"I can't believe I've worn you out so fast."

"A car that still goes at the end of a race simply hasn't been driven properly."

"I thought a carbon fiber monocoque was supposed to be indestructible."

"So that's why you wanted me to be Monocoque."

"The truth is, you are made of something softer," I said.

The jibe pricked him into action and, with just a modicum of encouragement from me, he proved once again that he was, indeed, my Monocoque.

"Will you be ready again for Hockenheim?"

"Germany, Hungary, Belgium ... all the way to Brazil," he said.

"Oh my, you've really caught the travel bug."

"It's amazing what a passion for sport can do."

And what a year of passion that was for me and my hard Monocoque!

PLAYING WITH THE BIG BOYS

LEXIE BAY

Playing with the Big Boys

Friday Afternoon – Sales Meeting

"We need this deal guys! I don't care which one of you gets it but I need it signed and on my desk ASAP! Jay Morgan is only in town for the next few weeks and then he flies back to London and we're done. Every agency in the city is after his business and I want us to be the ones to get it. Understood!?" Gary slammed his palm on his desk to emphasize his point. He was not one to hold back on his feelings when talking to his team, and these hand-slamming, chest-thumping speeches were a typical start to most meetings. Grace rolled her eyes.

She looked around the room at the rest of the all-male sales team. New York slicksters with the gift of the gab, they all thought they would be the one to close this deal. As the new girl, she knew she needed to be the one to do that. She had to make her mark to keep her place on the team, and as the only woman she needed it more than any of them.

Danny caught her eye and winked at her, flagrantly checking out her tits in a top that was perhaps an inch too low for business dress. She winked back and blew him a kiss while thinking "dickhead" to herself. Danny high-fived his buddies, Adam and Nathan. The three of them were inseparable and totally competitive. She admired their drive, to a point. But sometimes it felt like they'd ice their own grandmother and use the body to climb another step higher.

Still, they were smart and they were ambitious. Grace liked that, although she would never say that to their faces. She also had to admit, even more reluctantly, that they were all pretty hot, but she had to be careful. If she did decide to have some fun with any of these three, she had to make sure that work came first.

After a lot of banter and bullshit, along with some actual discussion about the current sales targets, the meeting finally wrapped up and she followed the terrible trio into the break room for some coffee. They were all boasting about how they would be the one to get Jay Morgan to sign with the company, shouting outrageous claim after outrageous claim, trying to be the one to be heard as they all tried to outdo each other. She couldn't help smiling at their enthusiasm, even if it was misplaced.

Grace had met Jay Morgan once before at a party and she didn't think he'd be impressed by any of them. To be honest, the first thing she had noticed about him was that he was undeniably handsome; tall, dark and the owner of a devastating smile. The next had been his complete focus and his total dedication to his business. She had discovered, with a little gentle flirting, that his only relaxation was golf, and this was where Grace knew she could get close enough to him to bring in this deal. As it happened, one of the most popular golf tournaments in the business calendar was coming up, and she knew that Jay would be there. The problem was, she couldn't play as well as most of the guys, which meant that these three blowhards would all be better than her. The more tips she could pick up between then and now, the better. And if she could get these three show-offs to show her a thing or two, she might have a lot of fun doing it.

Smiling sweetly, Grace took the cup of coffee Nathan had poured for her. He blushed and she tried not to giggle. He always maintained a careful facade of "the big man" but Grace could sense his vulnerability. She knew he was desperate to make this sale, freaking out about turning thirty in a month or so, and from the way he was looking at her she figured he hadn't been laid in weeks, maybe months. Adam walked behind her to get a cup and slapped her on the ass.

"What you up to this weekend, new girl?" he asked grinning as she flinched. Fucking asshole. Grace swallowed the insult and shrugged.

"Nothing much, what about you guys?"

"What, no dates lined up?" Danny leered at her. Grace shook her head as she pursed her lips to sip from the rim of her cup. They all watched her and she knew that they were imagining what else those lips could do.

"Nope, it's difficult to get to know people when

you're new to an area …" she said looking hopefully at them.

"We're playing golf tomorrow," Nathan said, jumping in. "And we're one short, you should come with us?"

Grace saw Adam roll his eyes, but this was exactly the in that she needed.

"Thanks guys, I'd love to. What time are you playing?"

"I can pick you up at 9:00," Nathan said blushing again. "We tee off at 11:00 but we usually get breakfast."

"Easy, Nathan," Adam said. "Offering the lady breakfast before you've fucked her? Don't you have that backwards?"

It was crude, but Grace and the others laughed at his quick retort. Still smiling, Grace took a step toward the door, considering an exit before crude banter unwittingly tipped into mindless misogyny.

"I hope you don't mind giving me some pointers as we go. I'm sure all of you are so much better than me," she said coyly, holding back her frustration at having to pander to their egos. Over her shoulder she added, "I'll try not to hold you up tomorrow!"

She turned down the corridor, straining to hear what they'd say in her absence.

"I'd like to hold her up." Adam said. "Up against a wall with my cock!"

They all laughed. "She gives me a fucken hard on." Danny said, trying to keep his voice down. "Her ass is like a peach!"

Grace pretended she hadn't heard them and kept walking, smiling to herself. Using these three to her own ends was going to be deliciously easy and, yes, she decided … it was also going to be a lot of fun.

Saturday Morning – The First Hole

"So here we are," Nathan said, smiling at Grace as she pulled her bag from the golf cart. "How about we check out your swing? Come up to the tee and I'll see what you can do, see if you need any tips on how to hold it."

"Watch out, he uses that line on all the girls, don't you Nathan?"

Grace laughed as Nathan shook his head. "Don't take any notice of Adam, he's just pissed off he didn't ask you first." Nathan picked up her bag and his. Then, with an unexpected display of tenderness, he suddenly took her hand and guided her up to the tee, while Adam and Danny wolf whistled at them both. Grace's heart was hammering in her chest. She hadn't expected him to touch her, and the warmth of his hand on hers was sending confusing signals to her core, signals that she hadn't felt in a while. He was so confident as he pulled her along behind him and all she could do was half run to keep up with him. She felt like a little girl, not a businesswoman trying to hold her own with the boys.

He put down both bags and let go of her hand briefly as he selected a club.

"Try this one," he said, then frowned, "although it

looks a little big, maybe we should have gotten you another set?"

"It's ok, I can handle the big ones," Grace said as he passed her the club, his fingers stroking hers as she took hold of it.

"That's good to know," he said, his eyes holding her gaze. "I've got another one you can try later."

Grace shook her head at the blatant innuendo. He winked and she blushed, stumbling backwards, surprised by how light the club was as Nathan released his grip on it. He grinned as he saw her surprise, "It's carbon fiber—top of the range."

"Very impressive," she said trying to regain her composure.

"It's not the only thing that's impressive, is it Nathan?" Danny shouted over, laughing as Nathan blushed adorably. Grace bit her lip and let her gaze run over his crotch.

"He's right," she said looking up at him. "It isn't the only thing."

"Um … should we do this?" He was flustered and she smiled to herself.

"Oh yes, I think we should," she said holding the club out in front of her.

Nathan raised a concerned eyebrow at her first attempt as he moved to stand behind her. He could hear Adam and Danny laughing at him, but the majority of his focus was taken by the sweet curve of Grace's ass rubbing against his thickening member as he leaned over her to correct her grip on the club.

-   "You hold it like this," he said, positioning his hands over hers. Grace closed her eyes, enjoying the warmth of his body against hers. He smelled just like he did in the office. He smelled like money and swagger and she wanted to sink into him and let him take care of her. Sometimes she wished she wasn't seen as the big ball breaker at every company she worked at. It would be nice to let someone into her life for a change. His crotch was pressed up against her ass and she could feel the thick length of his cock, hardening in his checkered trousers. Grace wiggled against him a little, leaning back against his chest as his grip tightened slightly on her hands.

"So, is my grip ok?" she asked, turning her head slightly to look up at him. Their faces were so close she could have kissed him and she felt his breath hitch in his chest. His cock twitched against her and she could feel him lose concentration as he looked down her cleavage. She loved what she was doing to him, but if she wanted to take this further, she needed to get him alone.

"You, uh, yeah, it's good but you need to spread your legs a bit wider for me."

Grace stifled a moan at the words he used. At that moment, in the warm sunshine, she could think of nothing she would rather do than spread her legs for him. "I can definitely do that," she said, easing her legs apart and rubbing against his crotch again.

"Good girl," he whispered against her cheek as he

leaned down to check her grip. "You look beautiful in that position."

Grace's nipples hardened as his breath warmed her ear. She almost forgot where she was as she imagined him saying that to her as she lay spread-eagled on his bed and he stood over her naked. She could feel the muscles of his arms where they wrapped around her, his strong thighs pressed tight against hers. She had a feeling his body would look amazing out of his crazy golf clothes.

"Come on Nathan, stop touching her up and show her how to hold your shaft." Danny nudged Adam, laughing as they teased him.

"You like touching my shaft?" he asked her, wrapping her hands around the club in the correct position.

Before she could answer he swung the club through the air, his arm sliding against her breast on the up stroke and grazing her nipple on the way back down. Grace whimpered, the noise half drowned out by the whistle of air as the club flew past her. She wondered if he could smell the desire radiating from her, the scent of her excitement bold in the fresh morning air. She wanted to turn around and kiss him but he had stepped back, leaving her cold, her body aching to feel his touch again.

"Try it again, but on your own this time," he said, "I'll watch you. I like to watch."

Grace shivered with anticipation, sure now that he would make a move if she could get him on his own. She swung the club, trying to remember how he'd done it.

"Not bad for a beginner!"

"Yeah, babe, you're a natural at handling his shaft." Adam winked at her and she smiled at him. He wasn't as cute as Nathan; not as tall and you could see the signs of too much easy living around his waist but he was lightly tanned with thick, messy dark hair and his accent was adorable, a little bit country and without that hint of ivy-league self-importance that Danny had. She looked over at Danny. He was still hot, even with that air of smug arrogance. In fact the arrogance might actually be what attracted her to him. She imagined him ordering her around in the bedroom. He was probably into spanking and other dominant stuff, and that thought only enflamed her desire further. She wondered what it would be like to fuck all of them.

"I've had plenty of practice," she called over. "Thanks for that," she said turning back to Nathan. "Do you think I'll be able to keep up with you guys on the course?"

"I think you'll be perfect." He held her gaze again and the intensity of his eyes made her shiver with lust. She was under no illusion about what he was thinking about, and it definitely wasn't golf.

"I'm a very considerate teacher," he continued. "Maybe I could give you some private lessons?"

"Maybe. Or maybe you and the boys could all show me how to play?"

"That could work too."

"This game obviously keeps you fit," she told him, reaching out to stroke the powerful curve of muscle in his forearm. "Maybe you can give me a workout too."

"Oh I think we'll definitely do that," Nathan grinned at her.

Danny teed up and took his shot, hitting it wildly off line, much to the amusement of the other boys. Grace watched them all, a plan formulating in her mind that would ensure she not only sealed the deal with Jay Morgan but also had the craziest fuck of her life ...

Saturday Afternoon – The Eighteenth Hole

Grace was exhausted. Her arms and legs ached and her face felt flushed from the relentless heat of the sun, but she had managed to keep up with them. She felt ridiculously proud and, on top of that, she had managed to flirt with all three until she was fairly certain she would be able to put her plan into action. She watched them laugh and joke as they packed up their clubs, and she wished that she wasn't heading home alone. The flirting had left her needy and wet, a familiar ache which she would have to rectify when she got home. Not that she minded satisfying herself, but she had to admit that a hot, sexy guy lavishing attention on her body would be a lot more welcome right now. And after spending hours with these guys she really wished that Nathan was taking her out for dinner and then back to his place for a seriously kinky fuck. He was definitely the hottest of the three, but the other two definitely had other desirable assets she'd be more than happy to acquire.

"You coming for a beer in the nineteenth?" Danny

asked, slipping his arm around her shoulders and pulling her towards him. "You played really well. Maybe you can make up our foursome more often!" He winked at the others, allowing himself a lingering glance down Grace's low cut top.

"I'd love to," she said, smiling over at Nathan as she spoke. "It was fun playing with you boys. We should definitely do it again. Although I was sort of hoping that you'd all take me out separately and give me a little one on one training first, before we get together again for the re-match?"

"I'll definitely take you out for some one on one! How about tonight?" Adam helped her with her bag as they headed toward the clubhouse.

Grace shook her head. "Trust you to make it into something naughty, Adam," she said, pretending to be shocked.

"I'm free after work on Monday if you want some more practice," Nathan said, smoothly removing Danny's hand from her waist and taking her bag from Adam. "I was watching you as you played—I think I have some useful pointers for you."

"That would be great, Nathan, thanks," she smiled, as Adam and Danny made hilarious jokes about Nathan pointing his stick at Grace. Nathan grinned back at her and held her gaze just a little longer than necessary. As they headed into the clubhouse, Grace decided that she was very much looking forward to Monday.

Monday Morning – The Office

Grace finished her phone call with Jay Morgan just as Nathan wandered over to her desk.

"Who were you talking to?" he asked.

Grace shook her head. "Just an old account from my last job. Thought I'd try and get them to come over to us, but they were uncomfortable with it. Nothing important."

Nathan nodded. "How was the rest of your weekend?"

"It was ok, watched some TV, and did some laundry. Nothing exciting. To be honest, I needed to relax a little bit. I had a few aches after the game on Saturday." Grace laughed.

"Then I'll be more gentle with you next time," Nathan said. "We can take it as slowly as you like."

Grace shivered a little at the possible double meaning in his words. She would love him to come good on his word, but she had a feeling she would have to push it with Nathan. More than the others, he could be a little shy, so a helping hand might be needed for him later.

"Looking forward to it," she said as her phone rang again. "I have to get this."

"Alright, later." Nathan went back to his desk, and Grace watched him as she took her phone call. He caught her eye a couple of times and she couldn't help but smile.

Grace opened an email and her heart raced. Yes! Jay Morgan had confirmed. He would be at the tournament and he was happy to talk to her about collaborating. If she played this right she would have the deal in the bag, and both her job and (hopefully) her reputation would be secure. She'd be Gary's golden girl.

Monday Evening – Back at the Golf Course

It was starting to get a little chilly as Nathan and Grace approached the fourteenth hole, and the sun was starting to set over the trees. It was actually very relaxing to be out here, just the two of them, and Grace studied Nathan's body as he lined up his next shot. Her eyes were drawn to the curve of his gorgeous butt and it was only the immediate danger of a golf club to the head that stopped her stepping forward to touch it.

"Nice ass," she shouted as he swung, and he swore as the ball curved to the left.

"Oops," she giggled trying to see where it had gone.

She looked back and realized he was watching her.

"Sorry, that was mean of me … but you're winning and it's not fair!" she said.

Nathan didn't stop staring and she bit her lip wondering if he was really annoyed.

"Are you mad at me?"

"No, not at all … I was just thinking how beautiful you look with the sunset behind you."

Grace blushed as he walked towards her. He held her gaze as he slotted his club back into his bag. She couldn't bring herself to move away, the proximity of his body making her shiver, the smell of his aftershave making her melt.

"We're the last ones on the course you know. The

guys ahead of us will have finished by now."

"Yeah? Did you plan that?" she giggled, feeling suddenly nervous.

"What do you think?"

"Oh …" was all she managed before he leaned down and kissed her, his lips crushing hers, his tongue prising open her mouth. His hands were all over her and he pulled her tight against his body so that she could feel his hardness pressed against her thigh.

"Fuck, you're so gorgeous," he moaned into her mouth. "You've been teasing me all around the course with that sexy little dress."

As he said it, he slid his hand up her thigh and under the hem of her dress. Grace arched against him as his fingers discovered that not only was she not wearing any underwear, but she was also unrelentingly wet.

"Oh you naughty girl," he murmured against her ear, his breath tickling her as he nibbled down her neck and bit the soft skin at the bottom making her gasp. His middle finger traced the outer lips of her pussy, her wetness allowing him to slide easily up to her clit, the gentle pressure as he stroked and teased leaving her panting, her breathing shallow and desperate. All she could focus on was the lazy slide of his finger, holding her breath to see if he would take it further. Her legs were weak with lust and her knees buckled beneath her as she wrapped her arms around his shoulders, The shiny nylon of his shirt made it hard to hold onto him and, as he kissed her more deeply, she slipped and they fell to the ground on the border of the fairway and the rough, her fingers scrabbling to hold on to his shoulders.

"Ow," she giggled as she looked up at him, her skirt rucked up over her thighs leaving her exposed sex pushed up tight against his groin. His cock was rock hard and she wriggled a little, the sweet friction on her clit making her shudder.

"You like that, babe?" he asked, tucking her hair behind her ear. The soft gesture was so at odds with the way he spoke and his usual swagger. Grace felt her heart lurch and pulled back a little. She needed to focus on her plan. The last thing she needed was to fall for Nathan. Although, looking up into his soft brown eyes, she thought it would be very easy to do. She leaned up a little and gently pressed her lips to his.

"I definitely like that and I want more," she told him.

He closed his eyes and kissed her again, running his hand up her thigh and under her backside, pulling her closer to him.

"Take them off," she said, catching his bottom lip between her teeth and sucking it into her mouth as she tugged at his trousers.

"You want to fuck right here?" he mumbled, sounding a little surprised.

Grace let go of him, planting tiny soft kisses all over his mouth. "Why? Don't you? I thought that was what you had planned? You made sure we were the last ones on the course."

"I was just hoping. I didn't know if you'd go for it. I didn't know if you were … that kind of girl."

"Well I think you got your answer, so take off those crazy golf shorts. I want to know if you're wearing anything underneath."

Nathan braced himself on his palms so that Grace could undo him. She took in the glorious view of the taut muscles in his arms as he held himself up over her.

"Do you work out?" she asked, running her tongue over his bicep, tasting the salty sweetness of his sweat.

"Yeah," he growled as her fingers fumbled with his flies. "Want me to show you how fit I am?"

Grace knew that she shouldn't find his swagger sexy, but god he was just gorgeous. It was a long time since she'd been with a guy who was so sure of his sex appeal; and while she felt as though she was betraying womankind, fuck it, because she had never been so turned on. His smell was a wonderful blend of a light cologne, testosterone and pure unadulterated sexiness.

"Yes please," she whispered as her fingers slid inside his open flies and found his cock. She pulled back and smirked at him. "I knew you weren't wearing underwear. Your ass looked too perfect in your shorts." Wrapping her fingers around him, she heard him moan, and that sound made her pussy twitch. "Please," she whispered as he kissed her. She pulled his shorts down his legs with her feet and wrapped herself around him pushing herself up towards him.

He smiled down at her and she melted. She drank

him in, his face, his soft brown eyes, the adorable curl of his lips and the hint of stubble on his chin. She wanted to feel it grazing her inner thigh as he guided her to climax with his tongue. She whimpered at the thought, letting her hands wander over his back, closing her eyes as she pulled him down on top of her.

"You are fucking beautiful," he said, leaning up on his elbows and stroking her cheek as he kissed the tip of her nose. Grace could smell the grass beneath them as he gripped her wrists and pushed her hands above her head.

"Should we maybe take this into the rough?" he asked, looking around them to make sure no one was watching.

Grace shook her head. "No, I want you right here, right now. Please Nathan, stop teasing and just fuck me."

"You're so naughty," he grinned. "I like that about you." As he spoke he spread her thighs a little with his until she was completely exposed.

His cock nudged against her, and she wrapped her legs around his, drawing him tighter against her. Grace looked up at him, her eyes widening as he pushed slowly inside her. She hadn't gotten a good look at him but, my god, he was certainly living up to expectations!

"Ahhh babe, you feel so good … so fucking wet." He was mumbling; his breathing shallow as her pussy grasped at his length inside her, he kissed her neck as he pushed her arms higher. She felt totally exposed to him, arms above her head, legs spread wide to accommodate his muscled thighs. The sky was darkening; the threat of a storm on its way and the wind was picking up, sending leaves and dandelion fluff swirling around them. Nathan pushed into her slowly, his eyes closed, his brow furrowed with concentration. Grace watched him, her body reacting to his gentle pace. She tried to buck against him, urging him to fuck her harder but he opened his eyes, a soft grin on his lips.

"Oh no, baby, we do this my way. You chose the venue, now I'm choosing how to make you come."

Grace whimpered as he pulled out a little further than before and then slid his full length inside her. Every move built pressure on her g-spot and she grabbed at the long grass of the rough, desperate to rush into her climax. Oh god, he really knew how to make her squirm. She wondered briefly how many other girls he'd lazily fucked to what she was fairly certain was going to be a spectacular orgasm—if he ever let her come.

"I like how wet I'm making you," he said, "I think I need to taste you." As he spoke he kissed down her throat and continued over the soft skin of her breasts, his tongue circling a taut pink peak as he slowly pulled out of her. His hands gripped her waist as he kissed lower.

Grace held her breath, fingers now trying to find purchase in the short grass of the fairway as he licked and nibbled lower and lower, his hot breath skimming over her own modest fairway at the apex of her thighs.

"So pretty," he whispered, his lips grazing her flesh.

She spread her legs wider for him, loving his gaze on her, bringing out the exhibitionist she so often tried to hide. "Nathan." Her voice was barely more than a gasp as she waited for him to stop teasing her. Then his mouth was on her and she almost squealed as he stroked her pussy with his tongue. Fuck, he was almost better with his tongue than he was with his cock. He had her legs quivering as he lapped at her clit, and then plunged his tongue inside her nuzzling against her with his nose. He kept the pressure on in all the right places until she was nearly incoherent with pleasure.

"You're so fucking wet, baby, it's so hot. You're going to come aren't you?" he asked her as she ground herself against his tongue, pulling away from her and making her whine. She nodded, her fingers tangling in his short hair, trying to pull him back down onto her. "No, no babe, I want to feel you all over my dick, and I want to watch your pretty little face as I fuck you hard."

Nathan slid up her body, teasing her with the luscious feel of his tight muscles against her skin, until he was pressing her into the ground with his weight. He slid inside her again, his cock pinning her down. He kissed her hard, his mouth hungry against hers, their bodies slammed together as he fucked her, his cock stroking her inside as its root teased her clit with every thrust of his hips. The wind was stronger than before and she felt splashes of rain against her overheated skin. The scent of the grass mingled with the sharp tang of sex and she buried her face in Nathan's neck to breathe in the smell of his sweat and their fucking.

The rain came down harder, their bodies slipping in the saturated grass. Their skin cooled quickly, the rain making them slide against each other. Nathan held her tight against him, fucking her hard as she gasped and moaned and writhed beneath him.

"That's it baby, come for me," he growled, her breathing more and more ragged as her nails clawed at his back. Grace was almost there, right on the brink, desperate to fall over the edge while at the same time never wanting this incredible fuck to end. Nathan seemed to sense her holding back and pushed her back onto the grass, making it impossible for her to resist him. He thrust into her, his lips on her breast, licking and teasing, doubling the sensations running through her until her legs were shaking with the building tension. He nuzzled against her neck, whispering filthy words against her ear and with that she let herself go; there was nothing she could do. Her orgasm slammed through her, so intense that she wanted to scream but found herself completely unable to. She gripped his shoulders, holding him to her as pounded her into the sodden ground.

As she shuddered beneath him Nathan didn't stop, giving her no opportunity to recover as he continued to fuck her. She let her hands wander over his back, grabbing his taut buttocks and holding him deeper inside her. Every thrust made her pussy tingle, her clit so sensitive, her nipples still erect pressed against his chest. She wanted him to come, wanted to feel him let go and know that it was because of her. She could feel him tense and she gripped him tighter with her pussy, urging him on until he swore and, with her name on his lips, came hard inside her. She could feel him filling her, hot and hard and throbbing as he kissed her over and over.

They looked at each other, grinning from ear to ear, and Grace giggled as the rain continued to pour down over them.

"We better get going before someone comes looking for us," Nathan said kissing her again. "Let's go get dried off."

Grace held his hand as they walked towards the parking lot and wondered if he'd think badly of her tomorrow. She suspected that she was just another notch on his bedpost, but hopefully she'd be a memorable one. Depending on how this panned out, he might just be another notch on hers. She smiled to herself and gave herself a mental high five. He'd been just as good as she'd imagined and, with any luck, there'd be a repeat performance at some point.

Tuesday – The Office

Grace was alone in the break room when Nathan came through the door with Adam and Danny following closely behind. She prepared for the barrage of banter as approached, wondering whether or not Nathan had told them what had happened.

"Hey beautiful," he said as he came over. Danny winked at her and Adam high fived Nathan as he reached for a fresh pot of coffee.

He'd definitely told them.

"Hi guys," she said. "How's your day going? Sell,

sell, sell?"

"Yeah, I'm having a pretty good day today," Danny said. "But not as good as *your* day yesterday, I hear!"

Grace rolled her eyes. "Yes, ok, you obviously all know what happened. Thank you Nathan! Can we be grown-ups about it please?"

"I want to know when it's my turn to take you out for a little one on one," Adam said. Nathan frowned at him but he pushed his arm. "C'mon, Nate, don't be like that. Gracie said she wanted to play with all of us, didn't you? I say spread the love!"

Grace sipped from her bottle of water and smiled. "Adam, if you want to take me out on the golf course, I'm free most of the day on Wednesday."

With that, she turned and headed back to the office, leaving them to gossip amongst themselves.

Wednesday Lunchtime – "Sales Meeting" on the Golf Course

"Quick, in here!"

Adam grabbed her hand and pulled her inside the bungalow, shutting the door behind them. This place typically provided respite and refreshment to weary golfers halfway through their game, but the sign on the door clearly read: "Open on tournament days only".

"How did you get in here? Isn't it normally locked unless there's a big competition?" Grace looked at him, her eyebrows raised.

Adam waved a key. "It helps when the bar staff have a crush on you. I told her I needed somewhere to store my equipment."

Grace laughed out loud. "And she bought it?"

"Well, it's not entirely untrue. I'm definitely going to be putting my equipment somewhere in here." He winked at her and she groaned at the cheesy line.

"Well let's hope she doesn't find out which equipment you were talking about, or you'll never get served in the clubhouse again."

As she spoke, she began to unbutton her golf top, gradually revealing her bright red plunge bra beneath. Adam walked towards her and she backed against the bar.

"Wait there," she said, tugging at the soft fabric of her skirt and letting it slide down her legs to reveal a matching silk thong. The effect on Adam was immediate, and the bulge in his trousers twitched in response.

"Is it getting a little hot in here?" she asked, reaching behind her.

"What are you doing?" he asked, then jumped as she suddenly sprayed him with a blast of carbonated water from the soda gun. Grace giggled as he spluttered and tried to move out of the way, his white t-shirt turning transparent. He grabbed the soda gun from her and doused her with the cold wet bubbles, making her squeal.

"Adam, no, please," she tried to get away by jumping up on the edge of the bar but he wasn't going to show her any mercy. He sprayed the effervescent liquid between her legs and Grace moaned as the cool water soaked her silk covered slit and tickled against her clit. She spread her legs wider, settling herself onto the bar, before shrugging off her top, unclasping her bra and letting both garments fall to the ground. Grace palmed the soft flesh of her breasts, tweaking her nipples into hard peaks as Adam sprayed her chest and then aimed again at her clit. She squirmed as the cold water fizzed against her pussy, biting her lip and running her fingers down her body and over her soaking lips. Her clit felt hot and needy, and the soft silk suddenly felt like a barrier. Lifting one wet butt cheek and then the other, her silken thong diminished to a scrap as she eased it over her hips, down her legs and kicked it away. Now, completely naked atop the bar, Grace let her fingers roam over her body to all the points of pleasure she could find. Adam couldn't take his eyes off her as she touched herself, her hair soaked and plastered to her face and body, her skin glistening and her legs wide.

He unzipped his shorts and shoved his boxers down his thighs, his cock bouncing up against his stomach. Grace licked her lips, pushing two fingers inside herself, her breath catching as she found her g-spot. She gasped and braced her feet against a pair of bar stools.

Adam came closer, stroking his shaft slowly and deliberately as he watched her fingers fly in and out of her soft, pink pout.

"Allow me, babe," he said, "I know a little trick that will have you squirting like that soda gun."

He lay her down along the bar and slowly circled her

clit with two fingers, sliding up and down her pussy until her legs were shaking with anticipation.

"Please," she whispered, pushing herself towards his hand, desperate to feel him inside her.

Adam slowly slid two fingers inside her, pressing the heel of his other hand against her sensitive clit and resting his fingers on her stomach as he began pumping his fingers hard and fast inside her. Within seconds she was writhing and gasping beneath him as he slammed into her, his fingers stroking and probing inside, stimulating her g-spot with incredible precision. His other hand slid further down until two fingers were either side of her clit, stroking in rhythm with his other hand.

"Oh fuck, fuck, fuck ..." Grace moaned, her legs shaking and her body taut as the most incredible, powerful orgasm rocked through her, a stream of clear liquid shooting from her pussy just as Adam removed his fingers. She came hard, shaking and screaming as he slapped and rubbed her pussy and clit over and over, drawing another orgasmic convulsion and another hard squirt.

Grace lay back panting, her body flooded with sensation.

While she caught her breath, Adam bent his head between her legs and slowly and lazily lapped at her soaking slit, his tongue making her twitch over and over until she was desperate to feel his cock, begging him to fuck her. In response, he picked her up and bent her over the nearest table, pushing into her without waiting, her slick pussy accommodating him immediately.

"God, you're so wet …" He fucked her hard, making the table jolt upon the floor with every thrust. Grace couldn't speak, her orgasm still fluttering through her, Adam's cock pushing her closer to another climax. She reached beneath her and strummed her clit as he gripped her hips to hold her still.

"I wish we had some lube, sexy girl. Looking at your gorgeous ass is making me want to fuck you there as deep as I'm fucking your pussy."

Grace gripped the edge of the table, his words raising goosebumps on her skin.

"Me too," she groaned, "I love that."

Adam pulled her hair, lifting her head off the table and forcing her to arch her back, allowing him to enter her more deeply. She was so close to coming again, but she wanted to wait for him. Wanted to feel his cock pulse inside her as she came hard and rippled all over him.

He grunted as he ground against her, "Oh Christ, Gracie, I'm going to come … You're such a dirty little thing, you drive me crazy …"

Grace pushed back against him, clutching him with her inner muscles as she felt him tense and let go, just as she too tipped over the edge, throbbing around him, moaning his name as she collapsed onto the hard wood of the table. Adam lay on top of her, his heart pounding so hard that she could feel it through his chest.

He finally pulled out and stood up, helping her to her

feet. They looked at each other panting and smiling.

"Fuck ..." Grace managed. "That was unbelievable! Where did you learn to do that to a girl?"

Adam shrugged, almost blushing. "Saw it on a porno and thought I'd try it. It's not worked like that before, though. You really went for it!"

Grace grabbed a clean towel from a cabinet and attempted to dry herself off. She looked around. "We seem to have left this place in considerable disarray," she giggled. "Hope your friend behind the bar doesn't get into trouble."

They did their best to return the place to some sort of order, wringing out their clothes, mopping up the water and, slightly more sheepishly, Grace's squirt as best they could before Adam turned to her and asked, "Do you want to finish our game, or should we call it a day for the golf?"

"I think nine holes is enough for me today," Grace said, and smiled. "I'm not sure I've got the stamina for another nine."

Adam nodded. "Agreed. Let's go get a drink and relax a little bit."

"Are you going to brag about me too?" Grace asked as Adam checked the coast was clear.

"After what we just did in there, I might even brag to my mother!" Adam laughed.

"You guys are unbelievable," she said. "Give me a hand with my clubs?"

Adam effortlessly slung her bag over his other shoulder and she followed him, watching his ass as he walked.

Two down and one to go. She had them all distracted and she'd been talking to Jay all week. The golf tournament next week would just be her closing statement. She was fairly certain the deal was hers and, if she played her cards right, she would be celebrating in more ways than one.

Thursday Morning – The Office

Grace tried to ignore the banter as Nathan and Adam teased Danny about always being last. The satisfaction Grace got from playing (and playing with) two of these three guys definitely made her proud enough to brag but, at this stage, there was no one to brag to, and she thought it best if she kept her exploits to herself. It wouldn't look good for any of this to get back to Gary, and she really wanted a shot at Danny to see if he was as good as his friends.

It didn't take long for him to come over and chat to her.

"How's it going, new girl," he said, sitting down on the edge of her desk. Grace wasn't sure, but it seemed like some of the admin staff were giving her the evil eye.

"I'm fine, Danny, how are you?"

"I'm feeling a little left out, to be honest," he said, fiddling with some paperwork on her desk. "You've been playing with the others, but you haven't asked me to show you my game yet."

"When are you free?" Grace asked. "You only need to book a tee time if you want to show me your technique."

"I could probably fit you in after work tomorrow.

What do you think?"

Grace pretended to check her diary and nodded. "Tomorrow it is, Danny. I'll meet you at the course."

She watched him swagger back to his desk. Three out of three and just in time for the big tournament next week.

Friday, late afternoon – the Ninth Hole ... In the Rough

"Shhh, someone's going to hear us! I'm a member here, babe, I don't want to get thrown out, or seen."

"Well you should've thought about that before dragging me into the bushes and doing ... this ..." Grace was already enjoying the delights of Contestant #3, and she gasped as his fingers slipped deeper inside her. She let her head drop back, glad for the support of the large oak tree behind her as a half stifled moan escaped from her lips. Danny silenced her with his mouth, kissing her long and hard as he pushed his fingers deeper, searching for the sweet spot that would make her whimper again. He grinned as he found it and felt her legs buckle beneath her. Good thing he was holding her up with his other hand, pressing her against the rough bark of the tree. Danny knew just what the ladies liked and he intended to show Grace exactly what made him so popular. He'd had his eye on her since she started and he had to admit that he was a little pissed that Nathan had gotten there first. But what the hell, that just gave him the opportunity to show her she was wasting her time with the small fry. His sales figures were higher and his cock was bigger and he was fairly certain that Grace would be more than impressed. He'd certainly had no complaints from any of the other girls—inside or outside of the company. He let his thumb stroke across her clit, loving the little noises that she made as he teased her.

Grace was so turned on, the exhibitionist in her loving the fact that they could get caught at any moment. Danny was so completely not her type, but there was something to be said for a change of routine and oh-my-god he was good with his fingers.

"Please ... make me come," she moaned as he teased her over and over, "and then I'm going to beat you at this ridiculous game."

Danny laughed. "Just for being a little brat, I think I might leave you hanging until you come good on that promise."

He slipped out of her and brought his fingers up to her mouth, pushing them inside and making her taste herself on him. She pursed her lips to suck them, her eyes never leaving his, her tongue wrapping around each digit then smirked as he bit his lip.

"Don't play this Casanova routine with me," she said, fumbling with the zip on his shorts. "You want to fuck me just as much as I want you."

She palmed his erection to prove her point and he closed his eyes, trying to stifle a moan and failing miserably.

Grace slowly moved her hand down the length of his

velvet hardness. She bit her lip wondering if she'd be able to accommodate all of him. He hadn't been lying when he'd bragged to Julie in Accounts about the size of his cock! She looked up and rolled her eyes as she realized he was looking smugly at her, nodding.

"Oh yeah, baby, it's just a big as they say it is!"

"Shut up you arrogant asshole and fuck me already."

As she spoke Grace pushed his shorts down to his ankles. He was circumcised, shining wet with precum, and she tried to wrap her fingers around him but he lifted her up, positioning her over the rosy tip of his cock. She wriggled against him but he held her tight, teasing her pussy, gently nudging at her soaking pout as she panted and clutched at his shoulders, trying to impale herself on his thick shaft.

"Tell me how much you want me," he growled as he lowered her slightly and her breath hissed through her teeth as she shook her head.

"No, you tell me how much you want *me*," she moaned against his lips, her fingers in his hair, pulling his mouth hard against hers, lips, teeth and tongues mashed together as Danny held her in place and thrust into her.

Grace's screams were muffled by his kisses, her body limp in his arms as he stretched her wide and obliterated any sane thought in her head. All she could think about was how good he felt inside her. She didn't care who heard them or if wayward golfers came looking for their ball. Her nails raked down Danny's back.

"Try not to leave any marks, babe," he grinned.

" ' Don't want my Saturday night asking awkward questions, do we?"

Grace was tempted to scratch him harder but she was distracted as his lips connected with her neck, kissing her softly and making her shiver. Her head fell back against the abrasive bark of the tree and she closed her eyes. His mouth was warm and soft, in contrast to his rough hands cupped over her ass as he pulled her down hard onto his cock and ground his hips, grazing his groin over her clit.

"You're such a dirty girl," he murmured against her lips, fucking into her hard, shoving her against the tree as she clung to his shoulders. "I want you to scream for me."

Grace was moaning as she bucked up against him, trying to match his rhythm, desperate to feel him against her clit again. "I want you to make me come," she told him.

Danny's legs were shaking and he stopped to take a breath. "I need to put you down, babe. I can't get as deep as I want like this." He lowered her to the ground and looked around them. "Perfect."

He kicked off his shorts and guided her over to a fallen tree, bending her forwards over it and spreading her legs wide so that she was completely exposed. Her fingers barely touched the ground and she tried to turn around to see what he was doing. Grace needed him back inside her, and being this exposed, her body prone and spread for him, only enflamed her need.

Danny knelt behind her and dipped his tongue into her waiting wetness, his fingers slipping around her waist and finding her clit, stroking gently as he fucked her with his tongue. She pushed back against him desperate for something bigger to fill her.

"You taste so good," he said as he lapped against her desperate pussy.

"I need you to fuck me," she gasped as her legs quivered with the strain of keeping herself in place.

Danny withdrew his tongue but, instead of standing, he traced further up with his tongue and she squealed as he connected with the pink pucker of her ass, probing her with the tip of his tongue.

"You like that, babe?" he asked and she nodded, unable to speak as he pinched and teased her clit, his tongue laving across her ass. At last, Danny stood up and positioned himself at the gape of her pussy, sliding just the stout head of his penis inside her.

"You're just a fucking tease …" she almost wept and then tensed as she felt his finger pushing where his tongue had just been.

"Relax, babe," he groaned, "I'm going make you come so hard you pass out.

As he spoke, he eased his finger a little further. Grace relaxed forward onto the broken tree and let him do what he wanted. His dick was stretching her pussy and, as his finger slipped in to the knuckle, she could do nothing but focus on the pleasure and the delicious pain that assaulted her limp body. In and out, his finger matching the rhythm of his shaft and, as he got faster, his other hand slipped down to her clit, holding her tighter to him as he found the little bud and stroked. Grace moaned and bucked as he drew her closer to orgasm.

Danny watched her, slowing his strokes as he sensed her getting close. What a fucking view, her perfect little ass stretched around his thick finger, her pussy clutching at his cock, the skirt of her little dress rucked up to expose it all, and the smooth, tanned flesh of her lower back. She was totally lost in the moment, abandoned to the absolute pleasure that he gave her, and it made him so hot to see her like this. He wished that he could see her completely filled—front and back, top and bottom—and he idly wondered if the other guys would be up for a little foursome. The only thing hotter than fucking and fingering her like this would be if one of the boys fucked her mouth and one fucked her ass while he pounded that adorable little cunt.

Grace gasped as she felt her orgasm build. In the distance she could hear voices and she wondered if they'd be discovered just as she came. She imagined shocked and scandalized faces, unable to turn away from her naked body spread out over the fallen tree as Danny filled her from behind, his naked ass pounding into her. Thinking about being watched pushed her over the edge and she wailed as her orgasm took hold, her legs stiff and her body tense, her pussy pulsing around his thick cock and her ass gripping his finger. Danny didn't stop, his strokes on her clit softer and lighter as she convulsed around him, panting and trying to catch her breath. He fucked her harder and deeper, pushing her into the tree trunk, eventually removing his finger from her ass so that he could grip her hips and hold her steady.

"Oh yes, baby, that felt *so* good," he moaned. "You like that, huh? I made you come hard didn't I?" As he spoke he slammed into her and she felt him start to tense up, his cock jumping within her. "Oh Jesus, fuck …"

Danny tensed up, his body pinning her down hard as his cock twitched and Grace felt the warmth of his cum as he unloaded inside her. He slumped over her and tried to catch his breath, his face close to hers.

"You're fucking awesome," he said, slowly standing up and pulling out of her, wiping his cock on the golf towel he'd grabbed from his bag and mopping her pussy so that she could get dressed. Grace stood up, a little unsteady on her feet and looked for the panties she'd discarded so carelessly a while ago. Danny picked them off a branch and waved them at her. She giggled as he threw them over and tried to step into them without falling over. He wrapped his arms around her and held her steady. She leaned against him, his body solid and reassuring and he kissed her on the forehead.

"That was a pretty incredible hole," she said smiling at him. "Let's see if you're that impressive around the rest of the course."

◇◇◇

Back in the clubhouse Danny bought her a drink. "A perfect round, Gracie, but you know, I think we should play in a foursome again some time."

"I'd like that," she said, her pulse racing and her nipples hardening as she considered Danny's proposition. "I was hoping you'd all be interested in teaching me a lesson again."

"I'll speak to the boys," Danny smirked, "I'm sure we can sort something out soon."

Grace sipped her drink, a wicked glint in her eyes as she thought about exactly what Danny was driving at. She had known he would be on the same page as her, she just hoped the other two would be as interested. Adam was a fairly safe bet, but she wasn't sure if they'd be able to persuade Nathan. Although it hadn't taken much to get him to take her on the golf course, she wasn't sure if he was going to be as keen to share.

The Morning of the Match

On the day of the tournament, Jay Morgan arrived as scheduled. Grace made a point to speak to him as soon as she saw him. She was certain that he would appreciate the direct approach, instead of all the testosterone fueled posturing that he normally had to put up with.

"Grace! Fantastic to see you again. How's the new job?"

Grace filled him in on how fantastic the new agency was, name dropping some of their bigger clients to impress him. They were deep in conversation when Danny and Adam came over to interrupt.

"Gracie, bad news, babe. The competition is a 3 ball,

so we took a vote and you lost. No hard feelings, but the boys gotta stick together if we want to win this thing."

Grace's heart sank. She needed to play today to keep herself in the picture and close the deal. If she wasn't on the course with Jay, the next time she'd see him would be in the clubhouse, and by then it would be too late. Someone else would have sealed the deal.

"Now wait a second, guys …" she started to say.

"Well this is perfect," Jay said. "Grace, we need a third for our team. My Sales Director let me down at the last minute. We were just resigning ourselves to a forfeit. You'd be doing us a favor if you joined us. What do you say?"

"Thanks Jay, I'd love to," she said, flashing a huge smile at Danny and Adam.

"The deal is mine!" she mouthed at them, loving their looks of disbelief.

———◇◇◇◇———

Five hours, a lot of talk and a few glasses of champagne later, Jay had agreed to go with Grace's company for his new campaign. She had his verbal agreement and an email to Gary to confirm the deal was theirs. Grace's golf, frankly, had been appalling, but she was on top of the world. Gary had promised her a huge bonus and the rest of the team were already talking about how she had managed it.

Jay shook her hand as he left. "Great doing business with you, Grace. Lovely day. I'll speak to you tomorrow to thrash out the details."

Adam, Nathan and Danny were torn between annoyance that she had beaten them and a twisted pride that one of their team had won the deal.

"Like you said guys, no hard feelings. Let me buy you a beer and then maybe we can ... celebrate?"

"Yeah?" Nathan asked. "What did you have in mind?"

"Well, I've got champagne back at my place. We could go and have a little party, just us four?"

"Fuck the beer," Danny said. "Let's take this party back to your place right now. I like champagne, babe, and I'm definitely up for ... celebrating."

Grace looked at the other two. "You ok with that?"

"Hell yeah," they said. "Let's go!"

◇◇◇◇

Grace opened the door to her apartment and led them into the open plan living room, before going to the kitchen to get a bottle and some glasses.

"Good work, boys," she said. "I have to admit I'll never be a golf pro, but the lessons were a whole lot of fun, and the Morgan account will be fantastic for the agency."

"You did a great job, Grace," Nathan said, taking the bottle and opening it with the skill of someone who did it on a regular basis. Grace watched the muscles in his forearms flex as the cork popped and a shiver of desire ran through her. There was something about closing a big deal that made her really horny, and she was hoping that the boys felt the same.

"Yeah, really nice work," Danny said winking at her.

She shoved him playfully letting her hand linger on his chest as she did so, catching his eye so he could see that it wasn't an accident. He grabbed her wrist and pulled her in for a hug letting his hands wander across her back and down to her backside.

"Hey!" she giggled, pretending to protest, while at the same time pressing herself tighter against his groin. She had a flashback to the golf course and to Dan's huge cock stretching her wide. She wondered how it would feel to have him in her mouth while Nathan filled her pussy.

Nathan handed her a glass of champagne, his fingers grazing Grace's as he held her gaze. Danny let her so that he could take his glass and Adam came up behind her, wrapping his arms around her waist.

"So, Gracie," Adam said. "Now that you've had all of us, which one is the best in bed?"

Grace laughed, "You sales guys are so competitive."

They all looked at her expectantly and she ran her eyes over each of them, as she pretended to think about it.

"You know, I couldn't possibly choose between you," she said. "I don't think it would be fair after having you all just once. Maybe I need to put you all through your paces together before I make that decision."

As she spoke, she slowly unbuttoned her blouse, revealing a jet-black satin and lace bra that hugged her curves, pushing her breasts up so that the soft flesh spilled over the cups. She shrugged off the blouse and tossed it onto the sofa. She stopped to gauge their reaction, smiling at their wide eyes and open mouths.

"Unless you're not up for that?"

"Oh hell, Gracie, we're more than up for that, aren't we boys?" Adam couldn't get his shirt off quick enough, looking at the others for confirmation that they were all going to get naked.

"We've talked about this at the office, but I never though ..." Nathan didn't even finish before his t-shirt was over his head.

Grace looked over at Danny and grinned. "You too, big boy?"

"Try and stop me," he said. "And get out of that tiny little skirt *now*."

Grace unzipped the skirt and let it fall to the floor, exposing a lacy black thong. She did a little twirl for them. "How's that?" she giggled.

"Yes, yes, yes!" Nathan moaned fumbling with his zip and pulling his pants off. His cock was rock hard, straining against the jersey fabric of his shorts and Grace reached out, running her fingertips up and down the restrained flesh, making it twitch as Nathan bucked against her hand. He pulled her to him, his lips finding hers, kissing her hard while Adam and Danny also stripped down to their briefs. Grace closed her eyes and let the sensation of Nathan's warm body against hers flow through her. Nathan's hands were on her waist holding her tight against him, and then someone else's hands were on her ass and someone was unclasping her bra. Nathan spun her around and pulled off her bra, freeing her breasts for Danny and Adam. Grace leaned back against Nathan and sighed as the other two lavished their attention on the heard peaks of her nipples. Nathan kissed the soft skin of her throat, his hand skimming over her stomach and down to the edge of her thong. She moaned, melting beneath the assault of their affections.

"I vote we take this to the sofa," Danny said, pulling back and pinching a glistening nipple between his finger and thumb, making her squeal. "I want to watch while one of these guys goes down on you."

They picked her up between them and carried her over to the sofa, setting her down and making her comfortable. Danny and Adam sat down on either side of her, and Nathan knelt on the floor between her legs, his hands on her thighs as the others took it in turns to kiss her, stroking her body, kissing and licking her breasts.

Nathan kissed slowly and teasingly up her thighs, and Grace felt as though the little strip of her thong was holding back a flood as she waited for his lips to reach their target. His fingers deftly slipped her thong to one side, liberating the syrup that the fabric had barely managed to restrain. Exposed to their gaze, she gasped, the heat of Nathan's breath making her desperate. He traced his finger over her lips, effortlessly dipping inside, his fingers nearly frictionless in her hot slick. Nathan bent his head and ran his tongue over her, his lips finding the hard bud of her clit and sucking.

Grace sighed as she lay back and let all of them pleasure her at once. So many hands and fingers and mouths. Her pussy was licked and fingered; her breasts were teased and tweaked, sucked and pinched. Nathan's dexterous hands pulled her thong over her hips and down her thighs so that, at last, she was completely naked, spread wide for their viewing pleasure and reveling in their ministrations. Nathan had two fingers inside her, massaging her g-spot, as Adam swirled nimble fingers over her swollen clit. Danny had produced a bottle of lube from a pocket and gently guided her just to the edge of the sofa where he was able to access the tight pucker of her ass with a slippery finger. She moaned as he dipped inside her, tensing then relaxing as he probed deeper.

She smiled to herself as she delighted in the adoration the three boys showed her. All of their bravado and posturing gone as they worked together bring her pleasure. Even now, Nathan and Danny were so focused on her needs that their foreheads nearly touched as their expert hands found her most intimate erogenous zones.

In time, Danny had one and then two fingers in her ass. First just the tips, and then deeper, stretching her wide as she adjusted to him. When she was as wide and slick as his fingers could make her, he sat beside her and lifted her onto his lap. He bent her forwards and Nathan held her against his chest as Danny probed her ass with the tip of his penis. Through heavy eyelids, she turned her head to see Adam stroking his cock. Nathan held her tight and safe, her breasts squashed against him as Danny positioned himself against her now soft and open asshole. He pulled her slowly down onto him, stopping as she tensed, and she gasped at the intense stretching as he pushed against the vulnerable ring of muscle.

"Slowly, babe, slowly," he murmured, drizzling more lube over his cock and around her opening. He eased her down again, pushing forward and, with a pop, his heavy swollen tip disappeared inside her. Grace moaned loudly as he slowly and gently thrust up into her ass, and Nathan held her upright as Danny sat back and let her lean back against him. His cock disappeared deep inside her and she gently bounced, using both Danny and Nathan for support.

Danny's hands roamed over her body, caressing her stomach and kneading her tits, pulling her back against him, giving Nathan perfect access to her pussy.

"We're all going to fuck you at once, Gracie," Danny growled into her ear. "Me deep inside your tight ass, Nathan in your sweet little cunt and Adam's going to fuck your pretty mouth. We're going to fill you up with jizz, babe, until it's spilling out of every orifice.

"Yes, please," she panted. "I want you to use me." They weren't the only ones who'd let go of their bravado. "It's all I've been thinking about. I want you to cover me in your cum, I want to swallow Adam's and then suck mine off Nathan's cock.

As she spoke, Nathan positioned himself between the two pairs of spread legs. Danny held her motionless briefly, still impaled on the formidable inches buried deep in her slippery rectum, as Nathan found just the right angle before plunging into her. He pushed in as Danny pulled out, gradually gaining speed until they were both pushing in at the same time. Grace was completely in their control, her body held still by Danny as they both fucked her, the sensation of two cocks inside her leaving her completely breathless.

"C'mon, Adam," Danny said, his voice strained with lust. "Her mouth isn't full yet." Adam stood on the sofa and straddled Grace, dropping to one knee as he slapped her cheek with his hard on. Grace ran her tongue over him, tasting his precum and licking up and down his shaft. She opened her mouth and he slid slowly inside. She could taste him, salty and sweet and she sucked, choking a little as he pushed deeper, his cock probing the back of her throat. She was filled completely, her body used by all three of them. She'd never felt so turned on as they slammed into her, her pussy, her ass and her mouth full; and she slipped her fingers down to her clit, stroking as they fucked her hard.

The sensation was overwhelming, and they were all clearly pushing themselves to the very limits of ecstasy. Danny came first, and she felt his heat filling her. But Nathan held on, pumping in and out, while Danny lay panting beneath her. He stayed deep inside her ass, hardly losing any of his mass even after his orgasm; while Nathan groaned, telling her how good she felt, how much she was turning him on and how he was going to come so fucking hard inside her. Her fingers flew over her clit and, just as Nathan reached his peak, his body tense, his cock pulsing inside her, Grace tipped over the edge, gasping, her pussy clutching at his dick, her ass rippling over the penis still buried inside, her orgasm shaking her whole body from top to toe.

"Fuck, yes!" Adam growled above her as he too shoved his cock in deep, coming in her mouth and then pulling out as she gagged and swallowed, shooting the rest over her lips and cheeks. As the streams of his orgasm abated, Grace licked her lips before doing her best lick clean the gooey cudgel of Nathan's spent penis. Once she had licked him to a sheen, Adam swapped places with Nathan. She was presented with the spoils of their mutual orgasm and, again, made to suck his cock clean.

Finally Danny slipped out of her ass and lifted her off him, onto the sofa. Grace lay there, limp and shaken with the aftershock of orgasm as they stroked and kissed her body.

"Wow! That was fucking amazing. I mean totally fucking incredible. Are you ok, Gracie?" Nathan was grinning as he leant over and kissed her lips. She wrapped her arms around his neck and kissed him back hard.

"I love you boys," she said. "But I'm exhausted and I really need a cool drink!"

"Yeah, me too," said Adam, getting up and pouring them all another glass of champagne.

Danny disappeared into the bathroom and emerged a few moments later with towels, cleaning up Grace as best he could. While Nathan thoughtfully went to Grace's bedroom to get a blanket and gently wrapped her up in it.

"Cheers, boys," she said, raising her glass to her

three naked colleagues. "Here's to us, to signing the deal of the month and to working and playing together again very soon!"

THE MASTER

MALIN JAMES

The Master

No one refused the Master. No one ever had.

In the midst of the Cold War, Alin Dalca had emerged from the mountains of Romania to revitalize sport fencing for a new generation. Then, suddenly, at the height of his career, he'd retired from public life.

Why, the fencing world had murmured, though no one ever asked. Dalca was developing a method. He needed privacy. Who was the world to refuse?

The fact that Dalca had not been seen in nearly fifty years had done nothing to dim his influence. Rather, his legend had only grown as he'd taken on students, one handful at a time, producing a lineage of athletes notorious for mental clarity and skill. In this way, Dalca had ceased being Dalca, and had instead become the Master.

Even now, with electrical scorekeeping and revised standards changing the sport again, to train with the Master was considered to be on par with Olympic gold. So when Tom Granger received an invitation to one of the Master's clinics, he accepted without hesitation, despite rumors and expense. The Master produced masters. That was enough for him.

At least, it had been back at his club in New York. It was a different story now that he was standing in a training room, naked, with three other men, in a remote château deep in the Italian Alps.

Tom watched the other men posture and stretch. They were familiar to him by name, though he'd only properly met one—the French national champion, Michel Bisset. Tom's mouth compressed. Yeah, he thought, as his eyes slid over the Frenchman. He knew him well enough ... The other two, however—a smooth, young Spaniard named Santiago Cerra, and a mountain of a Russian called Alexei Voloshin—were reputations and nothing more.

Tom rocked on the balls of his feet, pressing them into the fat, black line that ran the width of the room. They were all at their physical peaks; and yet, every fencer had a weakness to uncover and use. Tom's goal was to find theirs, without betraying his own. Of course, there was more to his interest than the bite of competition. Tom's sexuality, which could be best described as "omnivorous," was actively engaged in observations of its own.

Cerra's face had a sweetness that intrigued him. It made the rest of the package, from his shiny black curls to his boyish cock, all the more compelling. The Russian, on the other hand, was the Spaniard's foil. Whereas the Cerra was small and slender, Voloshin towered over Tom's six feet, and packed more bulk than most fencers preferred. And then there was Bisset ... Tom's jaw ticked, though his face remained still. Bisset always looked the same—flat muscle, quick hands, sharp, hooded eyes ... Bisset would never change.

The nudity had been the biggest surprise, of course, despite the first class tickets from New York to Milan and a château that looked like a miniature palace perched up on a cliff. After sipping brandy in the study, they'd been taken to a locker room that looked more like a Roman bath with its Aegean mosaics and white tiled floors. There, they were politely told to strip by an otherwise silent boy.

"Please," the boy said once they were all nude, "take medications and other necessities from your luggage and leave the rest here. All you will need is the equipment bags in your lockers. Retrieve them and come with me. I will take you to the training room."

That had been almost an hour ago. More than enough time, Tom thought, glancing at the clock set high on up the wall, to get the lay of the land.

The places he'd trained in were fairly industrial. Even Harvard's facilities could still be called a gym. The château's training room was something else entirely.

A wall of French doors opened onto a wide, railed terrace, (or would have, if it hadn't been twelve below zero outside), while full-length mirrors lined the other walls, so that the room and it's occupants spread out in all directions like precisely shuffled cards. It was oddly disorienting, like standing inside of a giant, glass box. Apparently, it had once been the grand ballroom of the château. At least whatever was going to happen was going to happen somewhere pretty, Tom thought.

Suddenly, the doors at the far end of the room opened and an old man came in, leaning heavily on a cane. A blonde woman followed him and quietly shut the doors.

The fencers jumped back into form like schoolboys caught out in detention—all except for Tom, who had casually kept his place on the fat, black line during the long, boring wait. It gave him the luxury of observation as the Master slowly approached.

He was small, Tom thought. Much smaller than he would have expected. But then, between nudity and mind games, (because that's what the hour spent waiting had been), everything about the clinic was miles from what he'd expected.

And then there was the blonde—an icy, blade of a woman with a sharp, sculpted face. Nearly as tall as Tom, and impossible to read, she walked one pace behind the Master like a personal guard. He had no idea who she was, but the fact that she wore the archaic black jacket and tight black trousers of a classical fencing instructor made him keen to find out.

The Master cleared his throat.

"Who do you think I am?"

The old man looked at them, head cocked like a drowsy owl. He could have been anywhere from sixty to eighty, and no taller than five-one—the pictured of aged authority addressing a clutch of supplicants. And yet, the wording of the question put Tom on guard. He smiled his affable, American smile and let someone else take the bait. He wanted to see how it played out.

"You are the Master, I presume."

Bisset …

Tom's face flickered before returning to neutral, while beside him the Spaniard shifted from foot to foot. The old man ignored them and smiled at Bisset. Tom had never seen a sweeter look on anyone's face.

"A reasonable presumption, of course," he said, in a soft Italian lilt. "I am an old man, yes? Standing here before you four young titans. And yet, the Master I am not. My name is Georgio Donati, and this is my assistant, Elle Mason. You may think of Ms. Mason and I as the Master's gatekeepers. Or, perhaps the tip of his sword."

A ripple of unease passed over the line. Tom held himself still. Suddenly, something clicked.

"Excuse me, signor," he said, as curiosity overrode instinct. "Are you the Georgio Donati who beat Santorelli for the championship in '76?"

The old man looked at him, quietly pleased, as Elle Mason's gaze slid over Tom like ice cubes in a glass. Instantly, the warmth of Donati's gaze vanished beneath the precision in her eyes. They were beautiful and unsettling, pale as a snow leopard's and not quite human. Tom's gut twisted, but he held her gaze, waiting patiently for her to look away. When she did, he'd have sworn she was bored.

"Yes, Mr. Granger," Donati said. "That was I—great skill beaten by greater fortune. But now I serve the Master. I have worked in his tradition for over fifty years, and it has served me well—just as it will serve whichever one of you the Master selects to train."

"Wait," Voloshin interrupted, speaking for the first time. "Whichever *one* ... please, can you explain?"

"Yes, what is this talk of one," Bisset cut in. "And, if you are not the Master, who is teaching this clinic? Is this some sort of joke?"

Donati looked at Bisset, blandly ignoring the Frenchman's impatience.

"This is not the training. It is a trial. Only one of you will be permitted to train. You will work under myself and Ms. Mason for the next two days, at the end of which you will compete for the single position."

"We were not led to expect a trial," Bisset said. Tom could practically hear his brow arching. He could be such an imperious son of a bitch.

"Your expectations are yours to manage, Monsieur Bisset," Signor Donati replied. "You were one of four invited to the château. If you believed that meant immediate entry to the training, that assumption is your responsibility."

"Please," a soft voice said. "What are Ms. Mason's qualifications. I mean no offense, Ms. Mason, I only wish to know."

It was Cerra. The Spaniard appeared to be on the verge of saying more, but shut his mouth instead.

"None taken, Cerra," Elle Mason replied. "I completed the training last year."

Her voice was dark and brandied, and rough as a cat's tongue, with the type of British accent that you only hear in films. Everything about her was predatory and strong, from her long-fingered hands to the timbre of her voice. Suddenly, Tom had no doubt as to her qualifications, whatever they happened to be.

"Wait," Bisset said. "A woman trained with the Master?"

Elle Mason turned the full weight of her lazy indifference on Bisset, who, Tom reflected, had apparently decided to play the role of the French misogynist.

"Yes, Monsieur. A woman. And not the first.

"Enough," Donati said, tapping his cane. "If you've finished your questioning, Monsieur Bisset, a few things before we begin."

Donati's tone was mild and sweet, but the timbre of his voice landed with a punch. The little man was not to be fucked with. To his credit, this seemed to occur to Bisset.

"Of course. My apologies, Signor."

Donati nodded, slightly, before moving on. Even standing still, he seemed to be on the very edge of movement, regardless of the cane.

"You will be working in the preliminary basics of the Master's method," he said. "Only fencers with the highest aptitude are taken on. It is … intensive, and not for everyone. Ms. Mason, please explain."

Elle Mason nodded and stepped forward without, strictly speaking, appearing to move. Tom's awareness shifted, driven by a subtle twist of lust. Unlike Donati, she possessed a stillness that was unsettling in someone so young. Looking at her closely, Tom realized that she couldn't have been more than twenty-two or twenty-three.

"As Signor Donati implied, this is a rather unorthodox method. The goal is not to teach you technique, but rather to dominate your opponent—physically, mentally and emotionally."

Bisset nodded knowingly. Tom rolled his eyes. Bisset was good, but he was also wired tight. He could be played, just like anyone else.

"However," Elle Mason went on, "for all of the benefit, there is a price to pay. You must obey, without question, all instructions that you're given."

Tom's eyes narrowed. It was a subconscious reaction—the word *obey* had many implications ...

"Excuse me," Tom said, dulling the edge in his voice. "What, exactly, are we consenting to?"

Donati nodded sanguinely.

"An excellent question," he said, all fatherly sweetness. "Fencing is a sport, yes? If you lose, the only thing hurt is your pride. But it wasn't always so. This is good for civilization perhaps, but not so for the fencer. Without a sense of immediate consequence, the fencer can lose perspective. Pain, or the threat of pain concentrates the mind. Pain brings with it distraction and anger. By transcending distraction and anger, the fencer attains control. This training method is designed to instill a sense of consequence, while developing the ability transcend it."

"Yeah," Tom muttered, "that's what I thought."

"Mr. Granger. Something to add?"

Elle Mason was eying him. Her mouth had curved, sharp and cold as the moon. Tom gave her a self-deprecating shrug.

"No, not really. Just sounds like this method pulls from other disciplines."

"Everything has a source," she replied, before picking up what sounded like a well-worn thread. "To go back to the sense of consequence Signor Donati mentioned, you will be using weapons that draw blood, though in very limited amounts. And," she continued, scanning their naked forms, "you will be doing so without the protection of traditional gear."

Tom's cock stirred even as the rest of him tensed.

"Don't worry, gentlemen," Elle went on, "you will be required to wear gloves and masks. And you will also wear these," she said, holding up a small, hard leather pouch, "to protect your future children. We've no interest in permanent damage, but your bodies will be exposed, and you will be challenged with moderate pain."

"When you are not training," Donati continued, "you will wear nothing but a number painted on your chest, noting your status in the group. You must be exposed—to your egos, as well as the sword. We have only a short time in which to assess you. This is the most efficient route. Does anyone have any questions?"

Tom felt the others shift, weighing their options and very likely themselves. Tom stayed still, despite the strange, seductive weight of Elle Mason's feline eyes.

"Very good," Donati said. "If none of you have any questions, I must ask you for your answers. Gentlemen, what do you say?"

Bisset was the first to step forward.

"I accept your terms," he said.

Alexei Voloshin followed, wearing a hard cock and happy grin. Tom couldn't blame him on that count at least— he had one hell of a cock. "I accept as well," Voloshin said. "It is for only two days, yes? How bad can it be?"

"Brother, you have no idea," Tom muttered, stepping forward. "Signor Donati, I accept. At least I know what I'm saying yes to."

That left the Spaniard, whose tight mouth and dark eyes kept him fully contained.

"I too know what I agree to," Cerra said, quietly. "I accept."

"Good," said Georgio Donati, obviously pleased. "Now don your equipment and we will begin."

For a moment, they all stood there, like children afraid to jump off a pier. Huffing with sudden impatience, Donati tapped the floor with his cane.

"*Now*, gentlemen. Times passes. If you are not back in your places in five minutes, we will begin with disciplinary measures. Do not disappoint.

Steel edged Donati's sweet, caramel tone. They all heard it and moved to the side of the room where their equipment bags lay. With a sinking feeling in his gut, Tom considered himself and the rest if the group. They were all wrapped firmly in their egos. He had no doubt they would have to be stripped of that too.

Working quickly, Tom undid the cord on the equipment bag and examined the items within—a mask, gloves, and the odd little pouch Elle had shown them a moment before. Tom eyed the pouch distrustfully before loosening the nylon drawstring and lifting the bundle out.

It was a fucking codpiece. They could call it "equipment" all they liked, but it was as close to a codpiece as a jock strap could get, complete with an obscenely padded leather cup. The only thing it was going to cover was his junk, which he supposed he should be grateful for. Tom held it up by a buckled leather strap. It was going to chafe like hell. Still, it could have been worse. It could have been a cock cage. Now *those* were fucking miserable—he should know. He'd made his subs wear them often enough.

Feeling a little bit better about it, Tom shook out the jock strap and immediately felt worse. The cup was of hard, polished leather, while the "thong" was nothing but buckles and thin canvas straps. It was ugly and uncomfortable—perfectly designed to fuck with someone's head. Tom looked at the endless mirrors. The vain among them were screwed.

Tom thought of Bisset. Then his cock stirred and he sobered up. It would be hell if he got turned on.

Tom assessed his semi-erect state and made a mental note not to get hard.

"Yeah," he muttered, as his dick ignored him, "good fucking luck."

Between the blonde with the icicle eyes, the dicks on display behind him, and the fact that fencing and fighting always turned him on, he was as screwed by the cup as Bisset, albeit for different reasons. Bisset's ego would hate the indignity of it. Tom, on the other hand, wasn't worried about his ego. He just knew it was going to be hell if he got hard. *Fuck me*, he thought, unbuckling the straps. *It's going to be a long two days.*

Though he didn't like wearing the codpiece, Tom knew his way around arcane instruments of torture well enough to put it on. Interestingly, he wasn't the only one. Cerra fit himself into his like a pro, visibly relaxing as he did. Tom had seen that look before, always on subs right after the cuffs went on. He filed the impression away, and then looked at the other two.

Bisset was trying to buckle the cup without losing his suavity, which was standard for Bisset. The Russian with the massive erection, on the other hand, was struggling. Tom briefly considered giving the big man a hand just as Voloshin caught his balls in a strap. Then he decided against it. Tom was a nice guy, but he was a nice guy on condition, and he wasn't entirely sure how he wanted to play the game.

"Two minutes gentlemen."

Donati's voice echoed off the mirrored walls and filled the training room. Tom adjusted a buckle to keep the thing from smashing his balls, while Cerra took pity on Voloshin. Interesting, he thought, as the Spaniard tried not to stare at the Russian's hard ass. Then Tom headed to the line, ignoring a ripple of unwanted awareness when Bisset fell in behind him.

"Ah, gentlemen, well done," Donati said. "And your companions? What of them?"

Tom shrugged. "Voloshin was having some trouble. Cerra helped him out."

Donati nodded benignly. "How kind of Señor Cerra. And what about the two of you? Did you encounter any problems?"

Tom smiled displaying the straight, white teeth his parents had paid a fortune for. "Nope. Easy enough to figure out."

"And you, Monsieur," Elle Mason said, addressing Bisset. "Any trouble?"

"*Non.* Eh, no trouble," he said. "What about you, Mademoiselle Mason? No special equipment for you?"

Tom watched, fascinated. Rather than flustering her, Bisset's stab at dominance made Elle Mason grin.

"No, Monsieur," she said. "No special equipment for me."

"Pity," the Frenchman said, doubling down. "I'm curious as to why? Perhaps different standards for women?"

Tom looked away. Meanwhile, Elle Mason pulled a grease pen out of the pocket in her tight, black pants.

"No, Monsieur," she said. "I wear no special equipment, because I have earned the right to wear clothes."

As if to punctuate the statement, Elle Mason drew a big, black *4* in the center of Bisset's chest.

"Just as *you* have earned the right to wear *this*," she went on, circling the *4* like a merit badge and recapping the pen.

"Earn your way up from that," she said, patting Bisset's arm. Then she flashed Tom a wink and turned away.

Beside him, the Frenchman's hand twitched. Tom looked past Elle and didn't respond. He knew that wink hadn't been for him. Regardless of how he felt about Bisset, he wasn't Elle Mason's tool.

"Ah! And with seconds to spare," Donati said, as Voloshin and Cerra rushed back to the line.

Voloshin smiled. It was a charming, chagrined sort of smile, like the wagging tail of a St. Bernard who had eaten the Sunday roast.

"Apologies, Signor Donati. This equipment is new to me. Cerra was good enough to explain."

Cerra flushed, bright enough to show in the mirrors. Voloshin looked straight ahead.

"Well, then. Now that we are all here," Donati said, clapping his hands, "the trial begins. Kneel."

No one but Cerra moved. Donati muttered something in Italian.

"*Por favore*, the rest of you. KNEEL.*"

Tom's scalp prickled. He could feel the old man pulling his strings all the way down through his spine. He didn't like it, but he knelt, as did Voloshin and Bisset.

"*Gratzi*. When you are not working, you will kneel, resting your buttocks on your heels, knees twelve inches apart, fingers laced behind you heads, arms perpendicular to the floor. This is rest position. Understood?"

"Yes, Signor Donati," the other men murmured. Tom nodded, unable to find his voice.

"Good. Monsieur Bisset has already earned his starting rank," Donati said, gesturing to the *4* on the Frenchman's chest. Bisset's face went gray. "However, the rest of you have yet to establish your places. Ms. Mason?" he said, bowing slightly to Elle.

"There are two halves to this exercise," Elle Mason said, moving to a rack of swords sitting flush against one mirrored wall. "The first is to breach Signor Donati's defense, and the second is to defend against my attack. You will do so with one of these."

Elle Mason stepped to the center of the strip, holding what appeared to be an old fashioned épée with an ugly, barbed tip.

"This weapon goes back to the days before electrical scorekeeping, when referees needed better ways to track points. In this case, spiked tips. It's a rough little thing," Elle said, pressing the pad of her index finger into the tip. Then she held up her finger, displaying a drop of blood. "They tear at padding," she said, ignoring the tiny wound. "They even penetrate jackets if the catch is nasty enough. Just imagine what they do to skin."

She sucked the blood off her finger with a smile. Tom's cock twitched, testing its confines.

"Will you and Signor Donati be using one of those," Voloshin asked, eying the épée's tip.

"I will be using one, yes. Signor Donati will be using this."

Setting the épée aside, Elle Mason pulled out a sharpened pencil and held it up. Voloshin laughed, a strange bark of disbelief.

"I cannot fence an old man armed with a pencil," he said. "It would not be right."

"It is not for you to decide what it wrong or right," Donati said, blandly.

"In fact," he went on, "I believe, Voloshin, that we will start with you. Select your weapon and meet me on the strip.

Obviously unhappy, Voloshin did as he was told while the rest of them watched Donati hand his cane to Elle. Then, shuffling slowly, the old man made his way to the Russian. Voloshin moved to help him, but Donati waved him off.

"The strip is my home, Voloshin. I am quite fine."

And surprisingly he was. Tom watched curiously as Donati settled into natural, loose-jointed, comfortable en-garde. Then he held the pencil up like a conductor and nodded to Elle Mason, who watched with narrowed eyes.

"En-garde. Ready. Allez."

Voloshin stood there, rocking back and forth, not making a move. Donati lowered his guard with a huff.

"Voloshin, if you do not do *something* you will find yourself tied with Monsieur Bisset for fourth place. Do I make myself clear?"

"Yes, Signor Donati," the Russian mumbled, before trying a half-hearted lunge.

"You attack like a twelve year old boy," Donati said, easily parrying the blow.

Voloshin thrust a bit more assertively this time. Donati blocked again. Tom cocked his head, watching Donati's static defense. There was no footwork, no aggression, no obvious avoidance, and yet Voloshin couldn't touch him no matter how he tried.

"End," Elle said. "Voloshin, to the side. Granger, you're next."

Red faced, Voloshin knelt as Tom rose and retrieved a weapon from the rack. Then, testing the weight and balance as he walked, he met the little gentleman at the center of the strip. Donati smiled and watched, rocking on the balls of his ancient feet.

Thanks to Voloshin's bout, Tom knew not to hold himself back, though he was careful not to thrust at full strength. However, he soon found his reservation to be unnecessary as well. No matter how he attacked—lunge, riposte, advance—he could not breach Donati's defense. His blade simply couldn't get through.

"End. Granger, to the side. Cerra, you're next."

Tom knelt again, curious and preoccupied. He couldn't see what the old man was doing—he only saw the effect. By the time Donati had finished with Cerra, and then, finally, Bisset, he was no closer to understanding.

Donati pocketed the pencil and brushed off his hands.

"Ms. Mason, would you bring me my cane," he asked.

"Of course," Elle Mason said, handing it to him as he trundled off the strip.

"*Gratzi, cara*. Now, gentlemen," he said, addressing the fencers. "You failed to get past an old man with a pencil. Perhaps you will do better against this girl's attack. Mr. Granger, you are first."

Tom stood, feeling all the more naked for the padded bulk of the jock strap as Elle Mason met him, fully clothed, on the strip. Tom flushed a hot, self-conscious red. It hadn't bothered him with Donati, but it sure the hell bothered him with Elle. The fact that suddenly his cock was hard enough to strain the confines of the cup only distracted him more. Tom struggled with his face, trying to keep it bland.

"All right, Granger?" Elle Mason smiled, thin and spiked as her blade.

"Sure," Tom said, with more bite than he'd intended. He was at a disadvantage and it pissed him off. "Whenever you're ready. *Elle*."

Elle Mason's eyes sharpened beneath lazy, narrowed

lids. Tom's body tensed. He'd misjudged and overstepped. Fuck it, he thought, as his balls tightened against the blunt rim of the cup. There was nothing to do but play through.

"En-garde," Donati said. "Begin."

Faster than he could clock it, she lunged, binding his blade when she could have easily taken the point. Unsettled, Tom tried to shake her off, but she bound his blade again. Again he disengaged. Again she bound. Again he disengaged. His temper lashed up as he threw her off, parrying with far too much force, but before he could riposte, Donati's voice rang out.

"Halt. Point left. Granger kneel, Monsieur Bisset, you're next."

Tom looked up, confused. He hadn't felt her score …

"Look where you're standing," Elle Mason said.

Tom looked down. She hadn't needed to score the point. She had driven him right off the strip. Tom's face burned. That hadn't happened in fifteen years. Impulsively, irrationally he stalked off of the strip, as the Frenchman passed him without a glance, dispassionate and cold.

Tom knelt stiffly as Bisset dropped into en-garde. Suddenly, he wanted to spank Bisset's ass redder than his own goddamned fucking face. The thought of the Frenchman bent at the waist, counting off strokes made Tom even harder than he already was, edging the chafe of the codpiece right to the edge of pain. It was that image that he focused on through the other three bouts, all of which ended in victory for Elle.

"Well," Georgio said, as Cerra, the final combatant, moved sanguinely off the strip. "Do any of you know why you failed?"

After an awkward pause, Cerra spoke up.

"Because we were distracted, and you were not."

Donati nodded, pleased.

"Yes. Precisely. You were all defeated because we saw you, and you failed to see us. You were too distracted—by discomfort, ego, pain, or anger—to effectively attack and defend. Consider what that means, gentlemen. It may help you come tomorrow. Now, for the initial ranking."

Elle Mason stalked the line, ignoring Bisset's glaring *4*. Voloshin received a *2* and Cerra the *1*, which meant that Tom received the—

"Three. Better luck tomorrow, Granger," Elle Mason said, dismissively capping the pen.

Tom's face hurt with the effort of keeping it blank.

Tom had been a top for nearly seven years, but it wasn't rope or humiliation that turned him on. It was bending someone's will, gently and subtly, so they didn't even know. That's what made him hard—discipline and control. He thought he'd had that mastered. Apparently, he'd been wrong.

He stayed in the training room long after the others, pacing the length of the strip. No matter how many times he walked through it, he couldn't see how she'd maneuvered him off. Where had the power tipped? In the end he had to conclude that it hadn't—she'd simply had it from the start.

By the time he got to the locker room it was empty, thank fucking god. Tom unbuckled the jock strap and threw it in his locker. His balls ached and his cock was sore from pushing against the cup—he was only a bit above average as far as size went, but his dick was just that hard. It had been since the bout. The fact that losing had turned him on made him vaguely sick.

Throwing his codpiece at the locker felt so good that he almost did it again, but he didn't allow himself. Instead, he took it out, folded it and placed it on the shelf like the civilized man he was. Then he took the hottest shower he could stand.

He cranked the water up, so the spray needled his skin and beaded over the 3. Relaxing into the punishing heat, Tom stroked his cock …

A thrill of filthy pleasure shot through him as he thought of Elle Mason, lean and feral, driving him off the strip.

"Fuck me," he muttered, and shut the water off.

No matter how badly he needed to, he didn't want to come—not thinking about that cold, cold blonde. The power dynamic was off. Somehow, in less than three hours, Elle Mason had fucked him up.

On the surface it was obvious. She'd played him on the strip without tipping her hand. His father would not be proud—Laszlo Granger hated a mark. The fact that there were witnesses compounded that shame. But still, Tom thought, he could have managed even that. Something simpler was fucking him up. Her prowess turned him on. He wanted her approval. He wanted to *please* her. That's what pissed him off.

Tom tossed his towel in a hamper.

What he really needed, Tom reflected, was to get his equilibrium back. Ideally, he'd have wrapped Elle's perfect ponytail around his fist and gently fucked her face. But that wasn't going to happen, and he needed an alternative that wasn't jacking off.

Tom walked over the heated tile floor into the adjoining dorm, looking for Bisset. It was a large, wood paneled room, lined with neat twin beds like a luxury barracks. At first Tom thought it was empty, but then he saw Cerra in the far corner of the room. His back was arched as he worked his cock with slick, fast strokes. Tom's attention focused, like a dog scenting a fox.

"Wait."

The word left Tom's mouth, driven by instinct, not thought. Cerra looked at him curiously. Then, with obvious effort, he did as he was told. Tom's shoulders relaxed. It wasn't what he'd been looking for, but it would do for now.

"Don't come. Not yet."

Cerra nodded again. Tom crossed the room.

"Did the session turn you on?"

He let the smile enter his voice as he sauntered to the bed.

"Yes," the Spaniard said.

He'd stopped just short of calling Tom, *sir*. Tom could hear the little word on the other man's tongue, ready to fall into the palm of his hand. But it didn't, and he was he was glad. He didn't need the responsibility. He just needed to get off.

"How badly do you want to come?"

Cerra looked at him, naked admiration softening his eyes. "Badly enough, Señor."

Tom glanced down at the cock in Cerra's hand. Precum coated its rosy tip, just beyond the reach of his thumb. His hand was trembling with the strain of not finishing the stroke. Yeah, Tom thought. *Enough.*

"And how much," he asked, "is enough?"

"Enough to earn it," Cerra said.

Tom gave him a Hollywood grin.

"Let's see you earn it then."

"*Si,*" the Spaniard murmured, soft and full of promise, like the inside of a mouth.

Tom moved to the edge of the narrow bed. Cerra sat up, gracefully swinging his legs over the side. Slowly, the Spaniard's hands drifted up Tom's thighs until they came to rest on his hips. Then, without preamble, he took Tom's length in his mouth, sucking and tonguing until Tom felt his cockhead bump the back of Cerra's throat.

Tom groaned, grabbing a fistful of curly hair, as Cerra worked his length with a hot, nimble tongue. *Enough* was more than enough. Tom gave Cerra's hair a tug and was gratified by the sweet little whimper that hummed around his cock.

Suddenly, Tom thought of Elle Mason's sharp, pale face. Rejecting the image, he steadied Cerra's head, thrusting harder and faster, until he hit the edge of his control. And yet, Cerra stayed latched on, working his dick with a highly skilled tongue while Tom failed to escape the vision of a sleek, blonde head.

Normally, Tom would have savored it. He loved the sound of whimpers and the clutch of fingers on his skin. But there was something inside him, something ugly and raw that needed getting out. Tom grit his teeth as it broke his control. He didn't want to stop, so he thrust with a violence that was nearly sadistic, until the orgasm poured out of him, into Cerra's hungry mouth.

"Do I interrupt?"

Tom opened his eyes as Cerra licked his swollen lips. Voloshin was standing just inside the door. He was smiling but there was a tightness to his mouth that Tom didn't like.

"Not at all," Tom said, squeezing the back of Cerra's neck.

The Spaniard's eyes were dark and unreadable, but there was a quirk to the side of his mouth. If he was worried about Voloshin, he wasn't showing it.

"In fact, I was going to go get some food," Tom said, disengaging Cerra and strolling towards the door. Whatever was going on, he hadn't meant to poach. He'd be damned if he got involved.

"Señor," Cerra said. "Do you grant me permission

to come?"

Tom glanced back. He should have remembered …

"Yes. You earned it well enough."

"Thank you, Señor," he said, soft eyed and sweet. Then he turned to Voloshin. "Alexei. Come here. You're late. "

Tom looked at Voloshin, who blushed like virgin bride.

"I said, come *here.* "

The Russian jumped in his skin. Then, with a sidelong glance at Tom, he did as he was told.

Tom's stomach turned as something in Cerra changed, unfurling and growing to fill the room. There was nothing of the boy about him now—he was a pretty-eyed demon with a closed, unreadable face.

Quietly, Tom left. The last thing he saw before shutting the door was Voloshin bent over the bed, legs spread wide, ass on display. The latched clicked just as Tom heard the crack of skin against skin.

For a moment, Tom stood there, unable to move. Then, with his back pressed against the wall, he slid down to the floor. He'd have bet money that Cerra was the purest of subs, not a switch with a huge fucking Russian ready to take it hard. He'd been miles off the mark …

Something was happening that he couldn't see, and because he couldn't see it, he'd missed something vital. Again. Which meant, Tom thought, closing his eyes, that he was wandering in the dark. Elle Mason, Cerra, his own arousal ... He had fallen off the map.

Though Tom barely slept, he woke up early and went to the training room well before dawn.

Slowly and methodically, he stretched his back, legs and shoulders, isolating muscle groups and measuring his breath until his body was warm and relaxed. Outside the French doors, snow mixed with stars in the fading night sky, though there was still enough darkness beyond the window to reflect the mirrored room.

Tom saw himself in the windows, pliant and strong— the man he gave lovers, his father, himself ... the man who'd fucked Cerra when he'd thought he was a sub ... the one and only man who had ever fucked Bisset.

Tom's mouth tightened. A habitual response. And then he thought of Elle.

She was so fucking cold, as cold as Bisset was hot. She was so cold that she burned, a blue flame in the night. He imagined the press of her body on the frosted window glass and the supple flex of her spine. Her eyes would flash, he thought, not with passion but impatience as she angled her hips and offered him her cunt. The thought instantly made him hard.

Tom rose from a lunge and leaned his head against the glass, stroking his cock as he did. He wanted to fuck that cold, white woman against a wall of ice and snow. He wanted the glacial cool of her body to thicken his blood and harden him like her. Tom stopped for a moment, cock straining in his hand, as the kernel of an instinct told him what he had to do. He could hear the truth of it, whispering and right ... *you must bend, bend, bend* ... But he wasn't ready yet. Soon.

He began to stroke himself again. He wanted so badly to come, but he didn't let himself. He hadn't earned it yet.

"Sorry, Captain America. Don't let me interrupt."

Tom's hand jerked as Elle Mason's reflection appeared behind his. He smiled and kept stroking his cock.

"Hello Ms. Mason."

Her eyes met his in the window, a cold level gaze, and he grew even harder, more ready to come. He was dancing on the edge. Slowly, he eased the pressure off his shaft, but he did not turn around.

Silence stretched between them, tensile and thin, broken only by their breath, as their eyes met in the glass.

"My apologies. I hope we are not late."

Cerra slid through the door wearing his sleek, submissive self, with a subdued Voloshin in tow. Using their entrance as a cue, Tom ambled past Elle Mason and knelt on the thick black line. Moments later, Donati came in, followed by Bisset. There was something bruised about the Frenchman that Tom couldn't peg and didn't quite like, something deep beneath the skin. He filed the impression away.

"Thank you, gentlemen, for being prompt. We will be pairing you off and moving you into different rooms for the first half of the day. But first, we remove your numbers, and start the day fresh."

Tom looked down at his chest. He'd forgotten about the *3* … Tom accepted the towel and acetone that Voloshin handed him. In two swipes, the number was off and his chest was clean. He passed the bottle and rag to Bisset, who took them without a word.

When they had all removed the signs of their rank, Elle Mason moved forward, smooth as spilled cream.

"Voloshin, Cerra, you will remain in this room with Signor Donati. Granger, Bisset, get your equipment and follow me."

Without acknowledging each other, Tom and Bisset rose and took a step.

"No. Hands and knees."

"*Pardon*," Bisset asked, voice sharp with challenge. Tom shook his head.

"I said," she repeated pleasantly. "Get. On. Your hands. And knees."

"I am not a hound, *Mademoiselle*."

Elle Mason smiled.

"Why are you here?"

Bisset stared at her, silent.

"Too proud to say," she went on. It was a statement, not a question. "I'll help you then. You are here in the hopes of training in a method you do not understand. Unless you've changed your mind, you will get on your knees, or you will leave."

"Jesus Christ, Bisset …"

Elle Mason cocked her head, and turned to Tom.

"Something you'd like to say?"

"Yeah, actually, there is ..." Tom gave Elle a slightly feral grin and launched his opening gambit. His instincts had been right. It was time to play the game. "Get on your knees, Bisset. We're pawns, and we're right where they want us. Isn't that right, Ms. Mason?"

Elle Mason smiled, in spite herself.

"No. Where I want you is five steps behind me, on your hands and knees with your equipment bags in your mouths. But yes. In the grander scheme of things, you are precisely where I want you."

A thrill of pure arousal slid through Tom's system. Jesus Christ, he wanted to fuck her. He wanted to split her wide open and pit himself against her will. He wanted to sink himself into her and absorb what she had—real, autonomous power. And the only way to get there was to maneuver and submit.

Tom knelt without breaking her gaze. Then he crawled across the floor to his bag. Face burning, he took it up in his mouth, but rather than fight the humiliation, he leaned into it and allowed his ego to squirm. Slowly, the heat drained from his face. He was calm and focused by the time he knelt five feet behind Elle.

"Very good, Granger," she murmured. "Monsieur?"

Grudgingly, Bisset crawled after Tom, dragging his equipment bag behind him like a sullen hound. Elle Mason's eyes flickered over them both. Then she turned and led them across the room as if she held their leads. Tom kept his eyes on the floor as she stopped before a mirrored wall. For a moment, she stood there, running her fingertips down one of the seams. Then she pressed it, and a door sprang open. Instinctively, Tom backed up, right into Bisset.

"Watch it, Granger," the Frenchman hissed, losing the bite he had on his bag.

Normally, this would have irked him—Bisset's irritation usually inspired a corrective response in him. This time he almost laughed. Bisset might have been a weapon Elle could use against him. But, luckily for Tom, he was as much a weapon as Bisset.

"Watch yourself, *slick*," Tom said, teeth tight around the strap.

A vein popped out in Bisset's temple, as Tom had known it would. Ignoring them both, Elle Mason snapped her fingers and led them into a dimly lit room. Tom followed, not quite at her heels. After struggling to get the strap back in his mouth, Bisset scrambled last through the door.

"Drop your bags. Wait in rest position there."

Elle Mason pointed to a line in the center of the room. This room was smaller than the main training room, but no less well equipped. With her back to both fencers, she flipped on all the lights while Tom waited patiently, trying to understand how she moved. He could anticipate most people, but he could not anticipate her …

"Put your equipment on," she said, selecting two swords from the rack. Her tone, Tom noticed, had lost its spiky edge. "I want both of you on the center line."

Tom found himself having a curious response to the change in her tone. Moving quickly, he put on the jock strap, ignoring his hard on and the ache in his balls, as he glanced over at Bisset. Gauging the man by his cock, it would appear he had shrunk beneath the pressure and the stress.

"Masks and gloves. En-garde position and hold."

Her command was voiced in a long, flat drawl, but beneath the boredom she was watching every move. Tom suppressed a smile. He was getting a sense for where things stood. Tom tightened a buckle on the jock strap and grabbed his mask and gloves. Then he met Bisset on the strip and sank into a loose en-garde.

To a stranger, Bisset would have seemed perfectly at ease, but Tom could see how tightly he was wound, from the tick in his jaw to the tension in his calves. The man nearly jumped when Elle Mason handed them their blades.

Unlike the weighted épée from the day before, the sabers she handed them were light and extremely springy, more like wire whips than swords. And yet these too had nasty barbed tips, in addition to sharpened blades. Tom's stomach dropped—he hadn't fenced saber in years.

Tom watched the smaller man flex his wrist, testing the weight of the blade. Bisset didn't like the saber any more than Tom did. For a moment, understanding passed between them. The jolt of connection thickened the air as thoughts of curved muscle and salty skin flickered over the Frenchman's face. Then Bisset broke the connection and Tom looked away.

"Don't worry, gentlemen," Elle Mason said,

addressing their unspoken concern. "You won't be fencing saber. These swords have a different purpose. The sabers I've given you have more whip than the weapons you're used to. For this exercise, your only task is to guard yourself from getting hit. Nothing is off limits, but there is a catch. You may not move your feet."

Elle Mason paused, smiling faintly while she allowed what she'd said to sink in.

"We must defend ourselves without footwork?"

"Yes, Monsieur Bisset. You are going to get hit, and it is going to hurt. Your task is to fence as effectively as you can.

"Now," she went on, eyes bright in her expressionless face. "Masks down."

Mind whirring, Tom lowered his mask.

"En-garde. Ready. Allez."

Tom had barely settled into en-garde when a blade whipped out and slashed across his torso. Hot, itchy pain crackled over his skin, but he checked the impulse to lash out. Instead, he shifted his weight and watched Bisset's blade spring back with more force than he'd expected. Taking advantage, Tom leaned from the waist and thrust, leaving a fat red welt on Bisset's chest.

"Good. Again. En-garde. Ready. Allez."

This time it was Tom who struck first, slicing through Bisset's parry with a vicious remise to lay a pretty stripe over his thigh. Following instinct, Tom struck again, striping the Frenchman's other thigh, to give him a matched set.

"One point per attack," Elle Mason said, suppressing

a feline smile. "Granger, where did you learn that control?"

Tom raised his mask and wiped the sweat from his eyes. It wasn't all that different from a quirt. "Practice," he said, dropping the mask back over his face.

"Fair enough. En-garde. Ready. Allez. "

And so it went, until Tom and Bisset were slicked with sweat and covered in angry red welts. Thirty minutes on, five minutes off, until both were trembling from the strain of maintaining a single position for so long.

"Enough," Elle Mason said, glancing at her watch. "Well done. Take off your masks."

Tom took off his mask and eased out of en-garde. His thighs felt like jelly and the cup had been chafing for hours. Challenges turned him on. He loosened the buckles a notch. Despite having received, on average, as many hits as Bisset, Tom was pleased with the results. The welts he'd given Bisset criss-crossed each other, deliberate and with style. His, on the other hand, were a ugly mess without precision or control.

"Granger. Well done. Bisset … you're going to want that on."

Bisset had taken off his codpiece and was breathing hard, more from stress than athletic strain. His balls, Tom noted, were tight against his body; his cock as hard as Tom's. He caught the Frenchman's eye, knowing full well what had turned him on. Bisset looked away and abruptly left the strip.

"Don't we get a fucking break?"

"Of course," Elle Mason said, ignoring Bisset's agitation. "Five minutes to stretch and hydrate. Then we begin the next exercise. After that, you get a break before the trial bouts this afternoon. You'll have the results by the end of the day."

Without another word, she was out the door. Tom smiled to himself. He was gaining a deep appreciation for the scene she was running. Still, there was Bisset ...

"You all right," he asked. The Frenchman had his back to the room and trembled like a racehorse.

"This is bullshit," Bisset said, without turning around. Tom nodded, oddly relieved by the arrogance dripping from his tone.

"I don't know," Tom said. "I assume there's a point to it."

Bisset made some sort of dismissive snort and faced him in the mirror. His erection had settled down a little, Tom was sorry to see. Much of Bisset was a mystery to Tom, but not his sexual wiring.

"This is not training. This is fraud."

"You can't really call it fraud. Besides, I thought you enjoyed learning new things."

Tom leveled Bisset a look, half lazy dominance, half thinly concealed sex. He wanted to see how he'd respond. Blushing until his cheekbones were as red as the welts on his abs and arms, Bisset simply shrugged. Tom's dick twitched in response.

He was about to up the stakes one more time when Elle stalked back into the room. He knocked back the last of his water, swallowing down half the bottle in one long, suggestive pull. Then he tossed the bottle aside and went back to the strip.

"No masks," Elle Mason said, as Tom picked his up.

"No masks," he repeated, hoping he'd heard wrong. "Ms. Mason, I'm willing to work with your protocols, but I don't want to lose an eye."

Rather than give him the cold dismissal he'd assumed he would get, Elle Mason looked right at him and smiled. Suddenly, she looked like Grace Kelly—soft and lovely and warm. Tom was fascinated by the change in her face.

"Don't worry, Granger. You won't lose an eye. We're using wooden épées with foam tips for this, and you'll be fencing at quarter speed. Wait for Bisset. I'll explain."

Warily, both men met at the center of the strip while Elle Mason brought two wooden épées down from the rack against the wall. Then she handed them over, first to Tom and then Bisset.

"The object here is to anticipate each other. Speed is not the goal. Observation is, so you will fence slowly, keeping time to this." She held up a small metronome and put it by the edge of the strip.

"When you read an impulse off each other," she continued, "I want you to say it. It could be mechanical, like "parry" or "riposte", or it could be emotional, like "frustration" or "fear." Don't think. Just say. Clear?"

"Clear," Tom said.

Something strong and sleek uncurled inside him. He smiled. He wanted to play.

"This is ridiculous," Bisset muttered.

"Then you are welcome to leave."

Elle Mason gave him a friendly smile. Bisset grudgingly picked up his codpiece and put it on. Then he met Tom at the strip and lowered into position. Not for the first time, Tom reflected on how obscene they must look in their bulging leather cups. And yet Elle Mason barely noticed, as if the sight were so familiar as to be hardly worth her notice.

"Heads are off limits," she said. "Everything else is fair game."

Then she bent and turned the metronome on, setting it to tick at a slow, methodical pace.

"En-garde. Ready. Allez."

Tom rocked back on his heels, thighs burning from hours in en-garde. The welts stung and his balls were sore, but while he mentally acknowledged the discomfort, he felt no attachment to it. His attention was on Bisset and the tick of the metronome.

Tom lunged. Bisset parried, as something old and edgy flared up on his face.

"What do you see," Elle said, as the Frenchman parried again and came at Tom with an aggressive riposte. "Anger? Frustration? Say it."

Bisset lunged and Tom counter-parried, slipping past the blade.

"You're struggling," Tom said without thinking.

"Be specific," Elle said.

Bisset flushed and attacked again. Again Tom

parried, before dancing out of range in time with the drowsy ticks, keeping his impulses measured. He wanted to go slow.

"Fear pulls your strings," Tom said, knowing, the depth to which it was true. Bisset lived in fear.

Tom advanced with a flèche, synching the shock of the movement with the sleepy metronome. Bisset tried to retreat, but Tom's sword landed squarely on his chest.

"Bullshit," Bisset said, breathing hard.

"Don't argue," Elle interrupted. "Bisset, what do you see?"

Tom stopped listening and attacked again, binding Bisset's sword. Bisset shook him off with a violent remise, opening up his flank.

"I see …"

Bisset shook his head, at a loss for words, just as the tip of Tom's sword glanced off his hip. The metronome ticked impassively beneath Bisset's ragged breath.

"Good. Granger, what do you see?"

Before Tom could respond, Bisset charged him corp-a-corp. It was an aggressive, desperate move. Tom angled his body, sliding against Bisset as he parried the Frenchman's sword.

"You're scared," he whispered, right into Bisset's ear. "You're scared and it makes you sick."

"What the fuck do you think I am scared of?"

Bisset advanced too quickly, nearly throwing himself at Tom. Tom backed up, giving himself the necessary space.

"You are scared of this," Tom said. Suddenly he

lunged, tapping the other man's codpiece, very gently, with his sword.

Bisset dropped his weapon as if he'd been stabbed. The sword clattered to the floor.

"Enough," Elle Mason said, picking it up. "That's enough. Break now. Be in the main training room in two hours. Well done, Granger. Bisset, cool off."

For a moment, she stood there, looking at them both, a queen assessing her knights. Then, looking preoccupied, she turned around and left. The door had barely closed behind her when Bisset stalked out. Tom hung back, giving him space.

He should have felt something—pride, satisfaction, sympathy, remorse … it was Bisset after all. But Tom felt nothing. Nothing at all, as he walked down the length of the strip, and shut off the metronome.

◇◇◇◇

When Tom entered the locker room, only Cerra was there, drying off.

"Where are Voloshin and Bisset?"

The Spaniard shrugged. "I do not know about Bisset, but Voloshin is gone. The method did not suit him, I think."

Tom nodded but didn't say anything. If Voloshin had left, there was nothing to say. Every man had to sort it out for himself. Cerra finished drying off and hung his towel up. Less than twenty-four hours before, Tom's cock had been down Cerra's throat. While his body wouldn't have minded an encore, the rest of him held back. It was odd, Tom reflected. The embarrassed, submissive boy was still there, twinned by the Cerra in front of him—a man with the poise of a cipher.

"Few people are what they seem," Cerra said, as if he'd read Tom's mind. "Voloshin was an exception. He lives on the surface. Better to leave than to push."

Suddenly, Cerra turned and held out his hand.

"Good luck, Granger," he said. The Spaniard's grip was deceptively firm, very much like the man.

"Thanks, Cerra. Good luck to you too."

Cerra smiled, his smooth, young face, unreadable. Then, without another word, he left the room. Tom shook his head. The whole exchange had been strange. At this point, he wouldn't have been surprised to find out that Cerra was the Master ...

The news about Voloshin had him vaguely concerned about Bisset, but he was nowhere in the showers , or the dorm. Tom shrugged, and headed back to the locker room to grab a cursory shower. There was nothing left to do. He might as well sit in the sauna and keep his muscles loose.

The welts on his chest and thighs had already begun to itch, but he ignored the discomfort as he opened the thick glass door, releasing a wall of heat and steam. Removing the towel from around his hips, Tom sat down and filled his lungs with thick, moist heat.

Despite the buzzing silence in the hot, little room, Tom could still hear the metronome ticking in his head. Experimentally, he ran a hand over his length. Running the second exercise with Bisset had been one of the hottest, non-sexual things he'd ever done. There'd been so many dynamics to play with, and all while Elle Mason watched, and pulled the strings.

Tom thought of the last time he'd seen Bisset. They'd been naked then too, though for entirely different reasons. He began to stroke himself. He didn't think of Bisset that often, but when he did, it always came to this—his hand on his cock and a chunk of lead in his gut. He'd taken advantage on the strip ... Tom leaned his head back and closed his eyes, breathing in the heat as his hand kept up the rhythm to an invisible metronome.

Wisps of cool air over his feet.

"Hello, Michel," he said, not looking up. "Close the door, will you. You're letting out the heat."

"Of course ... Tamás."

Tom looked up then. Only three people had ever called him by his given name. His mother, his father, and Michel Bisset ... and Bisset hadn't used it in a very long time. Quietly, he watched the Frenchman settle down on the bench across from him. The room was so small, the hairs on their knees touched.

"Voloshin's out," Tom said, leaning his head back and closing his eyes. His hand was still moving languidly over his cock. Bisset glanced down and shrugged.

"I'm not surprised," he said.

Tom paused, waiting for him to continue. When he didn't, he sat up and looked and at Bisset.

"I'm sorry about calling you out in there," Tom said.

Bisset raised a brow, looking narrow and cavalier. "No, you're not."

Tom smiled.

"You're right, Michel. I'm not."

"Why?"

Why …

The word was an invitation. Bisset always began that way. Inviting, suggesting … He left his aggression on the strip. Or at home, Tom supposed. With him, Michel liked to be taken. That's why they had worked, for a while, anyway. Tom loved to take.

"Because," Tom said, leaning forward. He could practically hear the other man's pulse. "I want to win."

Bisset's eyes shifted, before he covered up the hurt, which is what Tom had needed to see. The hurt was Bisset's key. Tom smiled, unlocking. Before Bisset could protest, Tom wrapped his hand around the back of his neck, and pulled him into a kiss.

Tom teased Bisset's mouth open, as the Frenchman stiffened and tried to pull away. Their kisses were always like that at first … Tom could barely stand it—the familiarity of it. He wanted to grind his hips against Bisset's and feel the man's erection rub against his own. But he held off, savoring the tension before the Frenchman relaxed, just as he knew he would. Then Tom slowly moved in, spreading his legs and moving forward on the bench, until their cocks stood beside each other, barely touching but hard as iron bars. Bisset groaned.

"There's something else," Tom whispered, dropping the words in Bisset's ear. The Frenchman quivered but didn't move. "I'm not sorry because you *need* this," Tom said, allowing his ego to push. "You just don't want to need it."

Bisset's breath went ragged as he pulled at Tom, scrabbling at the welts he'd laid over Tom's skin. Tom winced and grabbed his hand.

"Say it, Michel. What do you want?"

Bisset looked at him, dark eyes pleading and full of sex. Worry and sex. They were always paired for Michel. At least, they were with him.

"Say it," Tom said, not relenting for once. "Say it, or get the fuck out."

"I want this," Bisset whispered, trembling. He was so beautifully high-strung … Tom nodded, and kissed him hard enough to bruise.

"It's all right. I won't tell a soul," he murmured against Bisset's lips. "Your wife will never know."

Tom didn't like the bitterness in his voice, but he ignored it for what it was—old emotion. Nothing new. He grabbed a fistful of Bisset's glossy, dark hair, and twisted until the other man whimpered, sending chills over his skin, despite the suffocating heat.

"Come here," Tom said, drunk on the scent of Bisset's skin under the spicy expensive soap. The air grew even thicker. Bisset moaned as Tom slowly cupped his balls.

"Don't worry, Michel," Tom murmured, yanking his

head back while running a hand up the other man's cock. "This is what we do. Now get on the floor."

The classy thing to do, Tom thought, would be to go to the dorm and lock the door, but he didn't want to lose the momentum. Momentum was everything with Bisset, so he pressed the man to his knees, before following him down to the tiled floor.

"Hands and knees in front of me. Stroke your cock," Tom said, sounding, to his own ears, uncannily like Elle. "Get as hard as you can, but don't come without permission. Do you understand?"

"*Oui*," Bisset whispered, voice cracking. He was trembling again. The man was built like a greyhound, Tom thought as his cock stiffened even more. Tom reached around Bisset, deliberately running his nails over the welts that covered his ribs and thighs. The sound Bisset made was gold, a strangled protesting hiss. Tom loved that fucking sound.

Dripping with sweat, skin stinging, Tom prised open Bisset's crack to reveal his tight, pretty hole. Knowing that time was getting short, he sucked on his index finger and gently pressed at the opening, nearly groaning as he did. Bisset shuddered beneath him but didn't make a sound. Slowly the tight muscles gave way as if they recognized him, allowing Tom's finger to move smoothly in before withdrawing again.

"Don't stop. Don't fucking stop."

Tom smiled. Bisset was such a brat.

"What do we say," Tom said, withdrawing his finger and dealing Bisset a smack on the ass.

"Please," Bisset conceded. "Please don't stop."

"Better," Tom said, reaching for a pot of herbal balm sitting on the bench. He opened it and slicked his fingers with the sweet smelling ointment. Then he liberally greased Bisset's hole, before sliding his finger back in. Bisset shuddered. Tom smiled and joined the first finger with a second. Before long, Bisset was pressing back against his hand, keening and moaning like a proper whore. Tom's breathing tattered. Precum beaded the tip of his cock, drawn as much by the sound of the man in front of him, as from his own frustrated arousal.

"How close are you to coming," he said. He sounded breathier, more desperate than he'd have liked, but at this point, it didn't matter. Bisset was quivering under him, offering his ass like a girl at prom.

"I ... close," he said.

"Good. Hands off," Tom said. "Both palms on the ground."

Then he took Bisset's dick in his hand as he slowly guided his own cock into Bisset's eager hole. Tom groaned as the Frenchman's body slowly accepted him, clutching with desperate heat. Beneath him, Bisset bucked. Tom gave him another smack.

"Easy, Michel, I've got you," he said, his soft tone belying the sting of his hand.

Slowly, he set a rhythm, so and steady and painfully precise, like the metronome in his head.

"*S'il te plait* ... please. Please."

"Not yet. Don't come. Not fucking yet …"

Tom was pushing them right to the edge, but he was wanted to keep his control of Bisset right up to the end. Beneath him, Bisset thrust and struggled, unable to rein himself in. Finally, when Tom couldn't hold back any longer, he pulled out of Bisset and came, splattering cum all over the Frenchman's lean, gorgeous ass.

"Now, Michel," he said, panting. "Now come."

Immediately, Bisset came, wringing out his own orgasm as Tom milked his head. Then they both sagged onto the floor.

They were still sitting in the sticky puddle of their spend when the door to the sauna opened, revealing Signor Donati.

"Ah, good afternoon, gentlemen. Please, if you would clean up and meet Ms. Mason and I in the main training room as quickly as possible. There are announcements to be made."

Then Donati quietly shut the door.

Without saying anything, Tom lifted himself off Bisset and held out a hand to help him off the floor. Bisset looked at him, shattered and tempted. Then he shook his head and got up on his own.

"Thank you, Tamás, but no. This may be, as you say, what we do, but I don't have to like it. I will get up on my own."

Tom nodded. Grabbing his towel, he turned and opened the door. Then they both stepped out into the cold, over-bright room.

Nothing more was said, not as they showered or as they dried off. Tom watched himself and Michel as if through a distant lens. No eye contact. No conversation. No easiness. The habit of complication had reasserted itself. They were back to normal now. He was surprised to find himself feeling, finally, a twist of real regret.

◇◇◇

When they arrived in the main training hall, Signor Donati and Santiago Cerra were waiting for them beside the main practice strip. Cerra was clothed in traditional fencing gear. Elle Mason was not there.

"Thank you, gentlemen," Donati said. "Alexei Voloshin has withdrawn from the trials. What you may or may not have realized is that Santiago here has already finished the training."

Tom nodded. That explained a lot.

"He was kind enough," Donati went on, "to return and make a fourth this year, as we had only three suitable candidates. That means that you, Monsieur Bisset and Mr. Granger, are the only men left on the field. Ms. Mason has informed me of your progress this morning, and based on that, a decision has been made. All that remains is for this decision to be reinforced. It is up to you to either defend your position or change my mind."

"Where is Ms. Mason," Tom asked, sensing a set up.

"She is attending to other matters," Cerra explained.

"You will fence against me for your trial. Please, don your equipment."

Donati and Cerra waited patiently at the edge of the strip while Tom and Bisset put on the padded jock strap for what, Tom hoped, would not be the last time. Then, without acknowledging each other, Tom and Bisset, approached the strip.

"Standard épée rules," Donati said. "You will fence Cerra to five points. Monsieur Bisset, you go first."

Tom knelt, assuming rest position without a second thought, and watched as Bisset approached the center of the strip. To the unpracticed eye, he looked calm, but to Tom, he looked like a racehorse trembling at the gate.

"Masks down," Donati said.

Bisset and Cerra lowered their masks.

"En-garde. Ready. Allez."

Bisset and Cerra tapped blades, gauging each other. Suddenly, Cerra attacked at the mid-line, driving Bisset back. A fresh welt rose up on Bisset's shoulder.

"Point left."

Cerra and Bisset reset. Again, Cerra attacked at the midline, but this time Bisset parried and launched a running attack. Cerra retreated, but not quickly enough to avoid Bisset.

"Point right."

Tom narrowed his eyes. Cerra should have seen Bisset coming …

Rather than change tactics as one might expect,

Cerra attacked, once more, from the mid-line. By then, Bisset had caught on. The Frenchman parried and lunged. Then he attacked Cerra corp-a-corp for the point.

"Point right."

Rather than watch Bisset the next time around, Tom kept his eye on Cerra, who launched the same attack. Again, Bisset took the bait, scoring the point Cerra fed him. Now Tom was sure that the Frenchman was getting played, though he couldn't think why, unless as part of the test.

When the same thing happened for the final point, Bisset took off his mask, smiling like Errol Flynn.

"Congratulations, Monsieur Bisset. Your training serves you well. Now. Mr. Granger. Your turn."

Slowly, Tom rose and retrieved one of the barbed épées from the rack. His muscles ached, his welts stung and, save for the padded codpiece, he was as conspicuously naked now as he had been during his match with Elle. And yet, this time he didn't care. His attention was on Cerra. He wasn't going to be played.

"Gentlemen, en-garde. Ready. Allez."

Tom watched Cerra from behind his mask, allowing the Spaniard first attack. As predicted, he attacked from the midline. Tom parried, then countered with a lunge, easily scoring the point.

"Point right."

Tom's mouth compressed. It was bullshit. He wanted a proper match.

"En-garde. Ready. Allez."

Tom rocked back and forth, waiting for Cerra's attack. As predicted it came from the midline again. Offended, Tom swiped at Cerra's blade, beating it back once, before retreating a step—fencer for "fuck this."

Cerra paused and considered, before giving Tom a nod.

This time, Cerra launched an entirely new attack. It was an old variant Tom hadn't seen coming, though he was still able to parry and retreat. Nearly three quarters of the strip lay between them when Cerra lowered his guard. Relying on surprise, Tom launched into a flèche, scoring an honest point before the Spaniard could raise his guard.

"Point right. Well done, Mr. Granger," Donati said.

Tom nodded, breathing hard. Every instinct told him to fall back on decades of training, but he resisted the urge. Cerra was better, which meant he was going to have to gamble, not on the bout, but on the whole trial. The only way to win was to lose, and Tom was going to lose well.

"En-garde. Ready. Allez."

Cerra launched a series of rapid attacks, binding Tom's blade. He fought to disengage, but he couldn't stop Cerra from slipping in the point.

"Point left."

The final two bouts happened much as the third, with Cerra relentlessly binding his blade as Elle had, however, this time, Tom defended his position without stepping off the strip. Still, it was not enough to win.

"Point left. Match to Cerra."

Elle's voice echoed through the training room, as Cerra's point pierced Tom's skin for the third and final time. Tom ignored the pain as his head snapped up. He'd had no idea she'd been there.

"Well done, gentlemen. Masks off."

Tom pulled off his mask and looked at Elle Mason. She seemed brighter somehow, as if someone had turned her color up an extra notch. The effect was subtle and powerful. He had the sudden feeling that she had spent much of the past two days holding herself back.

"Excellent match, Granger," Cerra said, taking off his mask. Pulling his eyes off Elle, Tom shook Cerra's hand.

"Thanks," he said. "You too,"

"You both performed well, gentlemen," Donati said, addressing Tom and Bisset. "Alas, only one of you may train.

"Monsieur Bisset," he went on, "your victory is a testament to your training. You are a credit to the École and my good friend, Peidferre."

Tom waited for Bisset's ego to fill the space between them, but he felt nothing from the Frenchman, which was strange.

"On the other hand, you, Mr. Granger, are a credit to yourself. While Monsieur Bisset embraced his training, you abandoned yours and engaged your experience of the last two days. It was a valiant effort. Unfortunately, you lost."

Tom nodded, forcing himself meet Donati's eyes.

"And yet," Donati went on, "it is not the win that interests us, but the spirit, if you will. Which is why, taking into account Ms. Mason's notes and your performances here, we congratulate Mr. Granger on passing the trials. Tamás, you shall train with the Master, if you so choose."

For a moment, Tom stood there, unable to speak. Then, without pause or hesitation, Bisset held out his hand. There were two pink spots on his pale cheeks, but otherwise, he looked almost relieved.

"Congratulations, Granger. This method is not, perhaps, best suited to me. I wish you every luck."

"Thanks, Bisset," Tom said as, for the first time in years, he and Bisset addressed each other without subtext.

"Welcome, Granger," Cerra said, with a sly, playful grin. "Fencing you was a real pleasure. I look forward to doing it again."

"Yeah, me too," Tom said, distracted by Elle Mason's unreadable feline eyes.

"Come, Monsieur. Take that contraption off," Donati said, waving at Bisset's codpiece. "Join us for a brandy. You have earned it. As for you, Tamás," he went on, patting Tom's arm with a warm, arthritic hand. "The Master will see you soon."

Tom nodded. Soon Cerra and Donati had ushered Bisset out, and he was alone in the training room with Elle.

"You can take that off now," she said, facing the window. Beyond it, twilight was falling over the ice and snow. He knew without her telling him that she meant the training cup. He unbuckled it, easing himself out of it before letting it drop to the ground. He was hard, of course. Cerra, and even

Michel, hadn't gotten near to giving him what he actually craved—power. Real, instinctive, animal power. Elle had that power, and he wanted it. Even more than he wanted her. Without being told, he knelt in rest position, like the supplicant he was.

Elle didn't turn around. Rather, she slowly unzipped her jacket and peeled off her shirt, revealing the long expanse of her lean, muscled back. Tom's cock filled and lifted even more, until it stood hard, nearly parallel to his abdomen. Then she slipped out of her black breeches and turned around, framed by the mountains behind her, as naked as ice in the overwarm room.

"Who do you think I am," she asked, echoing Donati's question from the day before.

"You're the Master," Tom said, low and sure.

"Yes," Elle Mason said, walking towards him, pale and perfect, from the curve of her breasts to the narrow swell of her hips. "I am now. My father was the Master before me. I grew up in the tradition."

"Your name," Tom asked, hazarding the question.

"Eleanor Dalca," she replied. "Mason was my mother's maiden name."

All across her torso, arms and chest, a lacework of pretty white scars marred her otherwise perfect skin. Elle saw him look her over, and smiled.

"If you agree to train with me, you agree to certain things. Obedience, devotion, discipline, trust. Can you commit yourself to me?"

He looked up at her, at her feline grace and power, and felt himself relax as he gave her his strengths and weaknesses to eradicate and mold.

"Yes," Tom said, meeting her pale, blue eyes. "I can give you this."

He reached out, not tentatively, but with tremendous respect, as she allowed him to rest his head against the flat plain of her belly. Moving as if every inch were a granted permission, he pressed a kiss to the curls at the apex of her thighs. The skin beneath his fingertips was cold, as cold and hard as marble limned with ice, but beneath it there was passion, molten and strong. Tom lowered his head. Her core was liquid fire. With a sigh, she shifted, parting her legs so that his lips could find her wet, pink heat.

He lapped at her clit as her narrow fingers threaded through his hair, drifting and coiling gently. Then she grabbed a fistful, hard enough to sting.

"Good, Mr. Granger," she said, bending back his head and forcing him to look at her cold, impassive face. "Then let your training begin."

Also available from Sweetmeats Press

Janine Ashbless
FIERCE ENCHANTMENTS

Fierce Enchantments is a collection of ten short stories full of fantasy, magic and lust. Against the darkest and most perilous backgrounds, the blaze of desire burns even brighter. Erotica at its fiercest and most breathtaking! This book is part of Janine Ashbless' Enchantment collection, which includes Cruel Enchantment and Dark Enchantment.

"Fierce Enchantments is a vivid and diverse mixture of tales: kinky vampire hunters here, a re-imagining of ancient China there, a session of filthy fun in Camelot and much, much more."
Amazon

"The best erotic fairy tale writer around,"
Saskia Walker

"How one writer can produce story after story to such a very high standard is awesome—she puts other writers to shame. There are not enough superlatives to describe how I felt"
Jade: the International Erotic Art and Literature Magazine

Also available from Sweetmeats Press

Various Authors
WANDERLUST

Wanderlust is a portmanteau of erotic stories about travel, exploration and discovery. It is said that travel broadens the mind, quickens the pulse, and heightens the libido. So let the stories within these pages take you away!

The Passenger by *Annabeth Leong* – Suzanne is trying to escape her small town. But when she climbs aboard a truck full of captivating curiosities, she soon discovers she's not the only one trying to escape...

Packing Steel by *Lana Fox* – A jaded hitwoman is called out for one last job. But will she be able to make the hit if she falls in love with the mark?

Love Gun by *Fulani* – A traffic jam introduces Cerise to a steampunk craftsman. Turns out, he's recently made a Love Gun; and Cerise dares him to use it on her ...

Going Up by *Lily Harlem* – Faye has got herself a new man who takes great pleasure in introducing her to new experiences. A hot air balloon ride over the English countryside is only the start!

Heat by *Stella Harris* – A woman joins a volunteer group in Haiti. In the intense heat of the tropics, she lets down her barriers and discovers a lot more about herself.

Also available from Sweetmeats Press

Kyoko Church

DIARY OF A LIBRARY NERD

That's what this will be. A safe haven.
A place for no holds barred ranting.
A place for secrets. And drawing. Even if it's bad. Even if it's wrong.
No one will see here. No one will see this.
This is just for me.

Charlotte has secrets.

Charlotte Campbell no longer recognizes her life. Once a shy, married librarian, she now finds herself jilted, holed up in her deceased father's run down cottage, and demoted to working in "The Dungeon" with only an automated book sorter for company. Then there's the drawings she does. They are not what her work colleagues might expect. And there's Nathan, a young patron at the library—the reason for her demotion and the inspiration for her art.

When Nathan's emails reveal a startling truth, Charlotte discovers a new dimension of her sexuality. But unsettling dreams from her past continue to plague her and Charlotte is eventually forced to confront her most deeply rooted fears.

Part Bridget Jones' Diary and part Story of O, Diary of a Library Nerd is the Wimpy Kid for adults. Compelling, erotic and accompanied by the drawings from Charlotte Campbell's very grown-up mind, this private memoir of exploration and discovery is not to be missed!

Vanessa de Sade
IN THE FORESTS OF THE NIGHT

In the Forests of the Night is a darkly sensual collection of erotic fairy tales. Each story blends the magic and fantasy of the traditional fable with the carnality and lust we've come to expect from Vanessa de Sade!

In the timeless tradition of the storybook, each tale is vividly illustrated by Vanity Chase. Beautiful, visceral and devoutly debauched, Vanity's illustrations bring the book to life and explore a much more grown-up side of fantasy. The seven sexy stories within these pages offer up a mind-bending, pulse-quickening twist on a classic genre.

If you think you know how a fairy tale is supposed to end, this book will make you think again! Sexual and cerebral, magical and modern, In the Forests of the Night is the ultimate collection of sexy, adult fables!

CPSIA information can be obtained at www.ICGtesting.com
Printed in the USA
LVOW06s0416140815

449721LV00002B/1/P